T0156838

CABIN in the PINES. . .

and murders in the forest

Robert A. Busch

iUniverse, Inc.
New York Bloomington

CABIN in the PINES. . .
and murders in the forest

*This is a work of fiction. All of the characters, names, incidents,
organizations, and dialogue in this novel are either the products
of the author's imagination or are used fictitiously.*

iUniverse books may be ordered through booksellers or by contacting:

*iUniverse
1663 Liberty Drive
Bloomington, IN 47403
www.iuniverse.com
1-800-Authors (1-800-288-4677)*

ISBN: 978-1-4502-5602-5 (sc)
ISBN: 978-1-4502-5855-5 (ebk)

Printed in the United States of America

iUniverse rev. date: 10/15/2010

Dedicated to Leon Jaroff

CHAPTER ONE

"What's this crap?!" Frankie Salvo loudly questioned his wife, Lucy, as he held out a formal looking letter...which he had glanced at briefly after extracting it from the envelope.

She stared at him in disbelief; "How the hell am I supposed to know? You just opened it up," she fired back.

"Well I thought that you'd know, maybe expecting it; it's from your folks," he said as he continued to read. "It's a legal thing; looks like they want you to sign off on their cabin up north, that is if we aren't interested in it as part of your inheritance when they go. Where money is concerned, and this could be quite a sizable amount, your brothers and sister could suddenly become very interested, especially your brother-in-law, Dick. I don't understand how your parents, as smart as they are, could write this letter without talking to everyone first, or calling some kind of a meeting. I hope that they know what they're doing."

"Anyway, it looks like their lawyer wrote it up and your folks just signed it. Here, you read it; there are two pages, but the second one is the important one."

Lucy dropped the duster she was cleaning with and quickly grasped the letter. As she scanned it her dismay was obvious. "Well I'll be damned! I didn't have a clue about this Frankie, believe me. Mama and Papa never said a word about it; at least not to me. I'll bet that the rest of the family is surprised too, assuming that they all got the same letter."

"Oh they got it alright. See at the bottom of the letter; it shows that copies went to all of your three brothers and to your sister."

"I don't need another problem," Lucy sighed. "Why couldn't they have at least waited until after I have this baby?" She rubbed her big stomach gently, feeling the life within her that was only a few weeks away from making her and Frankie parents for the first time.

Frankie, although generally unemotional, looked at her with some understanding, but his Italian blood was still a bit rankled. "Don't let it get to you, babe; we need to find out more about what's behind this letter. We have to talk to Al, as the oldest in your family he may know more about it than any of the rest of us. Besides, he said, "he's the smartest in the group...next to me."

Lucy chuckled at that, feeling a bit better. "I can't argue about that. Now go bowling. You were on your way out when the mail came. I'll be fine."

Frankie gave Lucy a peck on the cheek and a quick pat on her butt and was out the door. Lucy sat down in her recliner, used the lever to release the back, then stretched out and closed her eyes. She thought about her parents, Emil and Rosemary, and how they had aged since she married Frankie, a mere four years ago. For some reason they had never really accepted him as part of the family, even though he was Italian. Al had said at one time that it was because Frankie's family came from southern Italy, while the DiBiasi families were Venetian Italians. But Lucy thought that there was more to it than that.

One thing she knew for sure that bothered her parents was that Frankie only went to church when there was a funeral or a wedding for a relative or friend; he was overtly antireligious. Lucy had learned to live with that, but Frankie's background was a bit questionable, she realized. Other than that he had been a good provider, and never denied her anything that she really wanted. Not to mention that the sexual attraction that brought them together in the first place continued as a major connection between them. Actually, there had been few points of friction during their four years of marriage. Lucy was very happy that Frankie was the aggressor in the family, and as rough talking as he could be at times, he was delighted when he learned that he was going to be a father.

He had always been reluctant to discuss, with any detail, however, what he had been doing for the years before they were married...his work, his education, or very much about his family, other than saying that most of them were still in Italy. She let it lie, obvious to his discomfort when such questions arose. She understood that he worked for some contractor, and always had a lot of free time. It all worried her, but she finally fell asleep peacefully thinking about the life moving in her stomach.

CHAPTER TWO

At the kitchen table, Emil and Rosemary DiBiasi sipped of what was left of their dinner wine. They never drank beer or whiskey, only red wine. Emil had made his own "Dago Red" for years, but had to stop a few years ago when his asthma caused him to have breathing problems. Now they drank the best Chianti they could find. They were financially comfortable in retirement; Emil had made good money as a construction supervisor, and he was receiving a nice monthly pension check, which started eleven years ago when he took an early retirement…at age sixty-four. He had felt healthy enough to continue working longer, and would have liked to, but Rosemary's arthritis had restricted her physical activity to the point where Emil was required to do more of the work needed doing around the house. They could easily afford to have a house-cleaning lady, even once a week, but they were somehow too proud, and they also cherished their privacy. Emil had once said to son Al, who had encouraged them to get some help: "I'd probably bust my bladder before I went to the bathroom with a strange woman in the house." The couple reflected old country modesty to an extreme. At least Rosemary's arthritis had stabilized; she could move around without much pain, but in rather slow motion. Her brain, however, was as agile as ever.

"Do you think we made a mistake, Emil?" Rosemary asked her husband. "I know we followed our lawyer's advice, but I still can't help but feel that we should have had a family meeting about the cabin first. I know I shouldn't, but I'll feel guilty about sending that letter if any of the family gets upset over it." Her dark eyes looked somber and her shaky voice affected Emil; he loved her and hated to see how she was aging. He had always worried that he would die first and leave her alone. She had said many times that she did not want to be a burden or have to live with any of their five children, except as a last resort, even though she knew that every one of them would readily take her in if necessary. Fifty-one years of marriage had brought the two of them to feel deeply about each other; there was mutual love and respect.

"I don't know, Rosie, but maybe it will all work out. We'll probably hear from the boys first, at least from Al. I don't want to talk about this over the phone; if any of them call, just have them come over. Maybe have them for dinner." Emil tried to put Rosemary's mind at ease, even though his own mind was troubled about the issue. He didn't say so, but he too, was beginning to doubt that the action they had taken was correct.

"We know how much they all enjoyed the cabin when they were growing up, and I suppose we both thought about who might really want the cabin when we go," Rosemary ventured, "but in some ways I thought they had kind of out-grown the place. That they would be into so many other things. They wouldn't want to spend their free time driving up to Munds Park, unless to go skiing. I doubt if any of them want to spend time maintaining the cabin. Maybe we'll be surprised and find out that none of them want it as part of their inheritance. They might just sell it and split the money."

Emil looked at his wife and could see the frustration in her face; she had never liked to have any disagreements in the family. He saw that if the questions in regard to the cabin were not peacefully resolved, it could be bad for her health.

5

"Well Rosie," Emil picked up, "there could be another problem, as much as I hate to mention it. If we find that no one is interested in the cabin and we can't tolerate the drive up there anymore, we may have to sell it. And that time might not be too far off. If we had to sell, the IRS would get a lot of money that should go to our kids. I would hate to see that happen; it would be a sin. When we had the cabin built, it cost us about $50,000; now it's worth about $400,000."

Rosemary looked at her husband in dismay, "I..I never thought about that; heaven forbid!" Her voice quavered as she nearly dropped her wine glass. "Isn't it possible to find someone to maintain the cabin for us? If we are still able to drive up there, it would be more enjoyable for us if we don't have to do any maintenance. Surely there are active, retired men in Pinewood or the RV Park who would be happy to have something to do when they're not playing golf, and make extra money at the same time." Her eyes brightened at the thought that somehow they could retain the cabin, at least for a while longer.

Emil became a bit perplexed; it was apparent that he really did not know what to do next; the letters had all gone out; it was too late to change that. He fell back on what he had said earlier. "Now we shouldn't get ourselves all in a knot over this; I'm sure that we will hear from Al soon, and then we'll set up a meeting with the whole crew of our kids. If they want to talk to their spouses later, that's fine, but I think that involving all of the in-laws right off the bat would muddy the waters too much. This has all got my brain spinning; I think that I need a little more wine."

Rosemary responded, "Me, too."

CHAPTER THREE

At the apartment of Jeremy DiBiasi, the youngest and only unmarried offspring of Emil and Rosemary DiBiasi, the phone recorder showed a blinking light, but he ignored it. Having just arrived, his first thought was to pour himself a glass of red wine, a daily routine upon returning home from work. He would have another later, with Maria from next door if she were to favor him with an evening visit, or he would have it with whatever he could scrounge up for his dinner. Having Maria in the room would postpone everything else, including the phone and dinner. He rarely dated on Friday nights; he was also a boxing fan and never missed a good fight on TV regardless of the weight class. Saturdays were when he went out on the town, often with one of the girls in the office at work. He knew that those that did date him always viewed him as a potential life-long mate, but they soon learned that he had no such intention; he enjoyed being a bachelor.

It being Friday night, Jerry could think of no better way, however, than to start the weekend with a visit from brown-eyes herself. He could easily give up the Friday night fights for another form of entertainment if she were to knock on his door.

He flipped on the TV to catch the five o'clock news, then plunked himself down in his recliner and sipped his wine. As a sales account executive, junior level, he had had a good day, closed on a healthy advertising contract that helped him pass his quota for the quarter, and he felt very relaxed. He reflected on his bachelorhood and that in all, it was not a bad life...except for the cooking part. His Italian mother's cooking had spoiled him and the care he received as the youngest son. His siblings all agreed that he had been spoiled, but his charm made them all love him anyway. That care had encouraged him to stay single and live at home, until his older brothers got him to understand that his care was getting to be a physical strain on his mother. He was a loving son, and finally realized that the things she did for him were, indeed, a physical burden for her, even though she never expressed a complaint about it. So he left, reluctantly.

With his wavy black hair, brown eyes, an athletic frame, and his well-paying Advertising job, his modest 5'9" body was no handicap in attracting very desirable young ladies. He even had had a brief fling with one eye-stopper beauty who topped him by four inches. She had worn flats on dates just to make him feel more comfortable.

Halfway through his glass of wine he decided to check the recorder; sort of giving up on Maria paying him a visit. He pressed the play button and heard his older brother's voice: "Hi Jerry, its Al. Trust that all is well with the young Lothario. Need to get together bro. Maybe you already know that Mama and Papa have tossed a surprise at us. Check your mail, if you haven't already done so, and call me, tonight if you can. If you are entertaining at home, I'll understand, so make it tomorrow morning."

Jerry hadn't stopped at the apartment's bank of postal boxes to retrieve his mail when he came home. Always in a hurry, he often skipped a day now and then to check his box, never expecting much personal mail anyway. He scurried down the two flights of stairs, ignoring the elevator, and pulled the box key from his pants pocket on the way down. He grabbed the small bunch of mail with one hand and snapped the box closed with the other. Taking the steps back up two at a time he was back in his apartment in almost a minute. Ruffling through the envelopes quickly, he dropped all but one official looking item on the entry table and tore off the end of the obvious one. Unfolding the letter as he read, his brow furled.

There were actually two pages to the letter; the first being a short letter from the attorney, Mr. Jacoby, merely explaining what he was asked to prepare for Mr. & Mrs. DiBiasi, and giving instructions as to treating the second page, which required a signature and a return to Jacoby. Signing the document was confirmation that Jerry had no interest in being part or whole owner of the DiBiasi cabin as part of his inheritance at the time his parents passed on.

Jerry stared at the form with a sad and perplexed look upon his face; the letter saddened him because he had previously not given much thought about the eventual death of his parents, and he was confused as to why they should have brought this subject to a head. He began to wonder if one of his brothers, or his sisters, were behind this weird action by his parents, or possibly his brother-in-law Frankie, whom he had never trusted. "Why would they do this?" he pondered; "They are only in their seventies," he continued to try and rationalize the action taken in his head, not understanding why they did not talk to him and his brothers and sisters before venturing into what he saw as purely a legalistic solution to their dilemma. His first thought was to call his dad, but he set that aside and decided to call Al; Al would know all about it, he was sure.

CHAPTER FOUR

Connie and Dick Horton drove into their garage late Friday evening, unaware of the stir generated in the family by "the letter" from Connie's parents. They were both worn out from the long drive from Los Angeles. When Dick shut off the motor he let out a deep sigh, "You know, Honey, I don't enjoy driving as much as I used to. I know that the west coast isn't all that far away, but for the twice a year or so that we go there, I think that we should consider flying in the future."

Connie had her hand on the partially open door, but stopped to reply to Dick, "We can discuss that option at another time, Dick, let's get into the house, but just let me say this: If you weren't so dang macho and insisting on doing all the driving, you wouldn't get so tired and bored with it. I do drive you know, and I am a good driver," obviously a bit miffed at her husband.

"Oh, hell, let's get out of the car; my butt's sore." As they entered the living room they spotted the pile of mail that had dropped through the door mail slot unto the floor. Dick said, "Let it be, Honey. Let's strip, put the clothes away, then sit down with drinks and see what's what with the mail. It's probably mostly junk anyway, that or a bunch of bills."

"Good idea," Connie quickly agreed. "I'll take care of the clothes while you put the mail on the coffee table and then fix the drinks...but put on your PJs first. I think that we'll be hitting the sack pretty soon...to sleep," she said with emphasis.

"We'll see," he said with a wink.

Dick stripped quickly in the bedroom and was into his pajamas while Connie was still hanging some of the clean clothes back into the closets and throwing those that had to be washed into the laundry hamper. With his Jim Beam and water in his left hand he sat in front of the coffee table and sorted through the pile of mail with his right hand.

The mail proved to be much as Dick had said, mostly advertising, catalogs, the usual solicitations from various charities, and two utility bills; a full three weeks' worth. As the couple sorted through it all, Connie picked up the only envelope that showed promise of something personal. "Hmm," she uttered; "this is from my Mama and Papa. That's strange; the only thing that they write us is cards for Christmas and birthdays." She opened the envelope as she spoke and then looked perplexed as she read the letter. "I don't get it. The envelope had my folk's return address on it, but this looks like it came from their lawyer and my parents." She was tired and her mind was not prepared to cope with legal issues. "What the hell are they trying to do? Cause a problem for the whole family?"

"Let me see that," Dick asked, simultaneously taking the letter from Connie's hand. He scanned the text quickly and then said, "Seems simple enough to me. I think that they are looking into the future, are conscious of their age and health, and are trying to settle some affairs ahead of time. Apparently they are also aware of the fact that their cabin in the pine country may be a problem between you and your siblings when they leave us. I suspect that there may also be some consideration of income taxes to be paid at that time...or if they wind up selling the cabin instead of it being part of their estate. Your folks are still sharp, Connie, and I suspect that they have been smart enough to get some good advice; obviously from their lawyer, Mr. Jacoby." Dick handed the letter back to Connie.

She scanned the cover letter from the attorney and then turned her attention to the second page. "Well," she said, "I'm certainly not going to sign this or anything else until the whole family gets together. I've got to know how everybody feels about this. The cabin is the biggest asset my folks have; it's worth twice as much as their home, or more. There is a lot to consider here, Dick; even though we are very comfortable, financially, and we don't have any children, doesn't mean that we don't care about what happens to the cabin. I'll bet all but Jerry are thinking that because of our condition, we'll just sign off on it. We have had some great long summer weekends up there with Al and Jean, and with some of our friends in the past. I don't see why we shouldn't be able to do that in the future. Right now I'm thinking that we could have a good co-partnership, or whatever, with somebody in the family. Don't you think?"

Dick nodded in agreement, also too tired to think seriously about anything. Although he was a small businessman, he dabbled in other things, and always seemed to know where money was to be made. "Come on, Toots, let's have our drink and hit the sack. We have a lot to do tomorrow. Our laundromat machines should be bulging with coins after three weeks, and there will be a bunch of bills to look over and pay. Don't worry about that now. Drink up."

CHAPTER FIVE

At his pharmacy, Gus DiBiasi locked up his cabinet of power drugs, as he called them, and shed his white jacket, draping it over his desk chair. A nervous tic caused his left eye to twitch just then, so he re-opened the cabinet and retrieved a small bottle. Removing the cap, he dropped one tablet into his left hand and quickly tossed the drug into his mouth, swallowing it without water. He locked the cabinet again, set the alarm system and exited the store.

In his car he felt somewhat relieved immediately; the frequency of the tic movement was slowed considerably. He hoped that it would be completely stopped by the time he got home; it really bothered his wife, Elaine, whenever she saw it.

"So far, so good," he said aloud to himself, but at the same time he knew that the only way to stop the tic permanently was to quit selling drugs illegally. It was not a wholesale thing, just to a few favored customers and one or two close friends…but it was a crime, and Gus was fully aware of the possible consequences. Elaine would leave him if she knew what he had been doing…he was sure of that. He knew, too, that she would take their only son, Tom; that was another risk he had been taking, and which added to his nervous tic. He needed to have his son, and was conscious of his son's need of him, as a father and fellow sports fan. His agitation was building over the situation; something had to be done. The extra money had been great, providing a wonderful lifestyle, which would end without the "side" money. While driving home he had time to also reflect on what effect it would have on his parents if they learned of his criminal activity; he thought that they would die of humiliation; they were proud people...especially his father. Elaine would have to forego her pricey clothes shopping, and probably cut back on her generosity to her many charities. "Oh hell," he thought, "forget it, it's cocktail time." He suppressed his concerns as he pulled into their circular driveway.

Elaine greeted him at the door with a drink in one hand and the letter in the other. "Here, my man, you may need this," she said as she offered the drink; "it goes with the letter." She gave him a quick kiss and patted his butt. At 41 she felt like 21, always ready for fun, especially the horizontal kind. Her Scotch blood was more than a match for Gus's Italian passion, which is what brought them together in the first place, and made it easy to overcome their religious differences. The DiBiasi family had reluctantly acceded to their wishes and they were married in a non-religious ceremony. Gus admitted to never having been a good Catholic anyway, although he did join Elaine at church every Sunday.

Gus took the letter and the drink simultaneously and plunked down in the nearest chair, taking a long slug of his scotch and water. Reading the letter over the top of his glass, he almost choked; "What the hell are they rushing things for?" he asked with an obvious tone of annoyance. "Why don't they just let us decide about the cabin after they're gone for Christ's sake!" The excitement caused him to cough nervously. He finished his drink and looked hesitantly at Elaine. "Get me a refill, Ellie; I can't shake this damn cough."

"In a jiffy," she agreed, "but don't let that crazy letter upset you anymore. I didn't expect it to trigger your tic again. I thought you had gotten rid of it with some of your super medications."

"Not to worry. I've got it under control." Gus replied, "Just give me that drink. See, it's stopped."

Elaine finished fixing the drink and handed it to him, but she was now more aware than ever before how less virile he had become of late. She was accustomed to their frequent visits to the bedroom, or any handy spot that would serve the purpose after the cocktail hour. Now Gus usually fell asleep for at least half an hour before dinner. She recalled how much they had always enjoyed each other during the long summer weekends, with their fourteen year-old daughter and son Tom away at summer camps; not anymore. She mused about the summers past and the pleasures they had brought, then decided to fix herself another bourbon and soda.

Gus turned on the TV and leaned back in his recliner as he finished off his second drink. "If I go to sleep, kiddo, wake me when dinner's ready," he said," or call Al and find out what's up with the folks." He went right to sleep.

Elaine let out a bored sigh and went into the kitchen. Perhaps it was time to get serious about the mutual sexual attraction she and her brother-in-law, Jerry, had been covertly developing. She decided that she would call Jerry after Gus was in bed for the night. Tuesday afternoon would be a good time, if it would work for Jerry, she thought. Her blood began to flow in early anticipation of the meeting, and she was thrilled when she did call and learned that he was as excited about having a tryst as she was. They agreed on meeting at two o'clock at a motel Jerry picked, saying that he would make the reservation. "Life doesn't have to be dull." She thought, with a smile.

CHAPTER SIX

Driving the few miles to the Twilight Motel in Mesa gave Elaine the time to think about what she was about to do. Her concern was what it might do to the solidarity of the DiBiasi family if the affair were exposed; she did not view that concern lightly. She loved her in-laws deeply, and had enjoyed time spent with all of the family members, except Frankie; she had frequently staved off his rough sexual advances. "We'll just have to be extra careful after this," she said to herself," especially when we're together with the family." As she neared the motel, her mind-set changed 180 degrees.

Elaine began to fantasize about Jerry, recalling how his brief but stimulating Christmastime kisses were during family celebrations. They were a tease for both of them, confirmed each time by a knowing look in each other's eyes. She began to worry a little: Would she be disappointed? Would he be disappointed? This was not going to be the teenage reckless passion thing where partner satisfaction concerns are out the window with all other caution. "At least we don't have to fuss with condoms," she thought," one benefit of no longer having any ovaries." She started to undress Jerry in her mind, picturing him naked on the bed, in full excitement, and awareness of her own body. She shivered and almost let go of the steering wheel; she felt her juices beginning to flow as she pulled into the parking spot in front of room #111, the number Jerry had told her would be open and available even before he would get there, which meant that she did not have to check in at the reservation desk, for which she was grateful.

Jerry had said that he would ask for a king-size when he called for the reservation, but the room was furnished with two double beds; Elaine wasn't about to create a problem; besides, she thought, it might even make it cozier. She and Jerry had been eyeing each other for months, touching hands and other body parts from time to time, discreetly at family gatherings. They were finally able to make plans to go further; this was it. It was 1:20 in the afternoon, and Jerry had said that he would be there at one. Elaine started to fret: "What do I do if he doesn't show?" she thought, "I'll just have to leave."

Just then she heard a car come to a stop near her door. Jerry parked his BMW next to her SUV and quickly came to the door. Elaine opened it as he entered. "Hello Don Juan," she said, greeting him with a full mouth kiss. He could only answer with an "Umm," followed by an "mmm."

Elaine released him a little, letting him come up for air. Smiling warmly, his eyes shining with a mixture of anticipated pleasure and the furtive anxiety of a man on the verge of entering into forbidden territory...his sister-in-law. Jerry quickly shared, "We don't have much time, you sex pot, and I'm sorry, but I promised to talk to Connie at three-thirty about the cabin, before Dick gets home. He gets an anxiety attack over anything having to do with money. She would prefer that he not get involved in the cabin problem; he's just too nervous. "

Of course, plans could change, and I might call her to set up a later date; it depends on how much fun we have here. Hey!" he said, "You're way ahead of me." Elaine had thrown back the spread on the one bed and was half undressed by the time Jerry stopped talking.

She shed her panties and bra as she slipped under the top sheet, which she had thoughtfully folded back. She lay there, eyes wide open, admiring Jerry's body as he unzipped and dropped his pants. His briefs soon followed. Elaine let out a gasp as she observed the gradual excitement building in his "extension." "Hurry," she urged, "Get in here before I erupt!" Jerry crawled in beside her, immediately smoothing his hand over her breasts and her erect nipples. He moved his mouth over her left breast and then over to the right one, then to Elaine's eager mouth. His right hand moved slowly down her torso until it reached a soft moist spot. Elaine shivered as he stroked her gently, while she reached between his legs and held his firm erection. Things moved swiftly after that; it was feverish and left them drained of emotion. They curled closely on the single bed, Elaine's eyes were shut, but she did not sleep. They both just rested for a while, neither felt like speaking; unexpectedly, Jerry started to get off of the bed.

"Hey! Don't go," Elaine pleaded, with an enticing smile, "Can't we talk a bit? We really should get to know more about each other, explore our desires. Maybe you'll feel like an encore. I wouldn't mind."

"As much as I would like to, sweetheart, I can't, I'm cutting it close now. This was great, though, and I hope we can do it again, very soon." Jerry said as he dressed. "Best if you call me to set up another time; no spouse to worry about on my side." He grabbed his keys and said, "Hate to make this short, Ellie; next time I'll try not to have a conflict. Take a nap, leave when you want to; the room's paid up, no need to go to the desk." He reached over the bed, bestowed a kiss on Elaine's eager lips and gently ran his hand slowly over her breasts. He went quietly to the door, winking as he left.

Elaine lay there, physically and mentally relaxed, trying to find justification for the affair, yet knowing that it was purely sexual, with no thought about what the future might hold for them, or what devastation it would bring to the whole family if and when it might be revealed. She knew that Jerry was a confirmed bachelor woman-chaser, but she now found herself attracted to him much more than before the tryst. Drifting slowly into sleep, a soft smile on her face, she started to think about when they could meet again.

CHAPTER SEVEN

"Sit down and eat your dinner, Al, I'm sure that Jerry and Gus will return your calls as soon as they can. They may not have even received the letter yet," Al's wife Jean suggested. "Even if they have received the letter, you should give them a little time to mull it over before you talk to them. I have a feeling that you, yourself, are not sure just what to think about it; I don't."

"You're right...you're right, Jean, but I've got to get a handle on this cabin thing before I call Papa. I really don't think that there is much of a question about how they will all feel about what Papa and Mama are trying to do, but then maybe I'll be surprised. I don't think that I can talk to Papa until I get some feedback on the letter, at least from Gus and Jerry. I've got to have some idea how they all feel about it before I call."

"I hope that Connie and Dick got back from L.A. last night, as they had planned. Dick is a good businessman and is always very logical; I value his opinion on almost any issue more than anyone else in the family. He may have a whole different slant on this thing than I do, but if he and Connie have gotten back by now, they might be too busy getting back into their laundromat business to give much time to the letter, maybe tomorrow. I can't wait too long."

Jean never let herself get unduly excited about almost anything; she had a Norwegian calm about her. Not a beauty, but she had a pleasant Ingrid Bergman look. Al always showed his pleasure when she stopped by the Post Office branch that he managed. Her short, bright blond hair always brightened up the room.

Al sat down at the table, but just started dabbing at his food, preoccupied with questions about the cabin issue and what his parents had in mind. His mind drifted back to his teens, a time when he loved to walk among the tall pine trees around the cabin, where he also would feed the squirrels...which often took the nuts right from his hand. There was no swimming nearby, but in the winter there was always plenty of snow for skiing and sledding. Then too, there were the wonderful long summer weekends together with some of the family going up Friday afternoons, leaving Saturday night, and others arriving then and staying until Sunday night. It had always been a great family time, with only Frankie being absent most of the time. It was so easy for everyone, what with the cabin only a two hour drive from anywhere in the Phoenix vicinity. ..with most of the drive on the I-17 freeway. At this moment he thought that his parents apparently never realized how much the cabin had been a major thing in his life, and probably in the lives of his siblings. It was something that he thought would always be a part of his life. What are his parents thinking of? They can't sell the cabin! They can't!

He came out of his reverie when Jean said, "Al, for God's sake, eat your dinner. Jerry or Gus could call any minute. You've hardly touched your plate." She had finished her own meal and started clearing the table, while Al continued to dabble at his meal. "Do you want me to stay home tonight?" Jean asked. "I don't really have to go to my investment club meeting; we're just going to pick a stock to study for next month. I'm sure that they can do that without me. I can mail in my monthly check to Betty, the treasurer, and I can call her now to tell her that I can't make the meeting."

Al looked up with a somewhat dazed look in his eyes, as though he wasn't sure of what she had said. "No, no, please go, Jean, and stay as long as you wish; I know that you like to gab with the girls after the meetings. No sense of us both waiting around for those phone calls; in fact, I might not wait anymore. I'm getting pretty antsy. As usual, with anything having to do with our folks, it will be on my back anyway. Connie and the boys will expect me to talk to Papa and Mama to get this matter clarified for everyone. So go!"

Jean grabbed her car keys from the plate on the table by the door, gave Al a quick kiss and was out the door. He speared a piece of meat without any desire to put it in his mouth; he was pensive, almost depressed. "It must be Mama," he thought. She was starting to show her age, more and more; he wondered if anything more serious had developed. He remembered that his uncle Pete, his mother's brother, had died some years ago from pancreatic cancer; the thought chilled him. "None of the others," he thought, "would know what's going on either; I've got to call Papa." He put his unfinished dinner in the sink and settled in his chair by the phone.

CHAPTER EIGHT

Emil answered the phone himself, with his usual, "Hello. This is Emil DiBiasi."

"Papa, this is Al. Can you talk?"

"Of course, Al. Why not?"

"Just wanted to make sure you were through with dinner; I know you hate phone calls during dinner."

"No problem, Al," he replied, but then said with some hesitation, "I suppose you called because of the letter."

"It is, Papa," Al responded. "I haven't talked to the others yet, but I am sure that they have received your letter by now and are wondering why you started up this cabin thing without getting us all together first. Have any of the others said that they wanted dibs on getting the cabin first? Is that what started all this?"

"I'm sorry, Al, we jumped the gun because of Mr. Jacoby, a lawyer friend; remember him? I'm sure you met him at one time or another, a while back. He closed his law practice, and is semi-retired, but I understand that he has a few old clients, like us, that he still does some work for. He dropped off some papers from his old office awhile back that he thought we should have, and we talked about the cabin. He said that because of our age we should start thinking about our estate, and he suggested that we find out which, if any, of our children would want to have the cabin, or be part owner of it, since it is a major part of our estate."

"But Papa, why didn't you get us together first? That is what everyone is probably most upset about; I know it is for me." Al was clearly bothered by this bypassing of the family members on a significant question. As the oldest son, he was used to being kept informed on almost everything his folks did. He felt shut out.

"Again, Al, I'm sorry," his father apologized, "because Connie and Dick were away, and Jake Jacoby wanted us to move on this thing, we agreed to his idea of finding out how you all feel about the cabin. Guess we jumped the gun. Probably should have just left it all to you guys to figure what to do with the cabin after we're gone."

Al went silent for a moment, not able to think about losing his parents. He loved them too much to contemplate their departure, yet he knew that what his father said made a lot of sense. "Okay, Papa, I understand, but I think that everyone would like to have a meeting first, before they sign off on the cabin, or whatever."

"That would be fine, Al. Would you be kind enough to do all the phoning, and set up a meeting here, maybe next Sunday afternoon? After church and lunch; about two o'clock would be okay."

"I'll be glad to do that, Papa, and I'll call you to confirm the date, or set another time if everyone can't make it next Sunday. I will suggest that only family members attend, not spouses, if you agree. Also, I don't think that Mr. Jacoby should be there this time; maybe later, at another meeting."

Emil was relieved that Al would make the arrangements, and agreed with the conditions he had suggested. He had realized that he and Rosemary had made a mistake in rushing forward with the sibling agreement, and now recognized that they were all likely to be upset, as Al stated. "Maybe it will all work out without any bitterness, with Al's help," he thought. "Thanks Al. None of you have to worry; you all know that whatever we do with the cabin and everything else, it will be handled in a fair manner for everyone. Call me as soon as you can about the date. Mama will worry about this whole business until we meet and clear the air." They said goodbye at the same time and hung up.

Emil walked into the sitting room where Rosemary was sewing, "Damn it Rosie, I guess we let Jake push us too fast on this cabin thing. Al is really upset, but don't worry sweetheart, he's going to set up a meeting with us and just the kids. He'll calm them all down, I'm sure."

Rosemary frowned, her dark eyes reflecting worry. "I hope so," she half whispered. "I don't want this cabin problem to create friction between the kids. I almost wish that we had sold it a long time ago, even if we had to pay some tax."

Emil paused in reflection of his wife's concern, his weathered face showing his own feeling about the situation, but he tried to show a positive attitude. "Relax Rosie, everything will work out, you'll see. Have a little more wine," he said as he poured her a half glass. She sipped it a bit, put down the glass, leaned back in her chair and drifted off.

CHAPTER NINE

Al had been able to establish an acceptable date for the family to all meet at the parent's home; it was Sunday, early afternoon; everyone arrived at or a little before the two o'clock time agreed upon. Although they were cordial with each other, there was not the usual jovial greetings that were always a part of the Italian family's custom. Emil did not offer the customary glass of wine to each as they arrived, knowing that it would be best to wait until the serious business was over. Only Jerry asked for wine, but Al suggested that they wait; Jerry did not argue.

"Papa asked me to get us all together," Al began. "This is our family; we are all equal here, so everyone should feel free to speak their mind. The subject, of course, is the cabin. I hope that no one will mind if I kind of steer the discussion. That okay?" They all either nodded or quietly voiced their approval.

"Before we begin," broke in Gus, "shouldn't Mr. Jacoby be here? After all, there may be some legal questions that need to be answered."

Al agreed, "You're right, Gus, there may be some legal hurdles to be jumped, and we may need Jacoby's advice later. I apologize; I thought that when I called each of you I said that he would not be here, just the immediate family members, with no spouses.

Guess I missed that in my call to you, Gus, sorry." Gus nodded in acceptance.

Emil interrupted with an apology of his own: "Mama and I are sorry that we started this situation over the cabin. I'm sure that Jake had our best interests in mind when he proposed that we get some agreement about the cabin now, instead of causing problems between all of you later. I think he was right, but we may have gone about it the wrong way and maybe too soon." He waved his hand at Al and said, "Go ahead son." Rosemary sat quietly, listening, but not happy with the progression of events.

"The first thing that we should do, I think," Al began, "is to determine the extent of any interest each of us have in eventually owning all, or part of the cabin. In responding in just a minute or so, keep in mind that the value of the cabin in the future." He paused, and said with almost a guilty look at his parents, "Maybe substantially higher or lower than it is today. The most recent guess at its current value is around $400,000, much of which has been generated by the escalating land value in Munds Park. Now let's get back to the question of interest, starting with you, Connie."

The oldest daughter, caught unexpectedly, stiffened up, her black eyes widened as though from fright. Although she and Dick operated their laundromat and dry cleaning business together, she always deferred to Dick on important matters. She hesitated to respond, but said, "I...I don't know. Dick and I will have to talk more about it, but since we have no children, and we like to travel, I think that Dick might agree that we would prefer my share in cash, but we will have to talk about it." She looked sheepishly at Emil and her mother, who had fallen asleep.

Al's brow furrowed in disappointment. "I had hoped that we could keep the spouses out of this, Connie, otherwise there will be too many opinions to cope with. Would you please call me tomorrow and give me your firm response? I would really appreciate that. Personally, I think that your response does make sense. Now let's go to our sister Lucy. How do you feel about the cabin?"

"Frankly, Al," Lucy said with a sigh, "all I can think about right now is having this baby." She patted her watermelon shaped tummy, and it was obvious that she would prefer to be elsewhere. "I understand what you are saying about the spouses, but you know Frankie. I'm sure that Dick will agree with Connie, but I have a feeling that Frankie would like us to own the cabin outright, or at least be a part owner. I'm sorry that I can't give you a firm answer right now," she said apologetically, "but I want to avoid any problems at home. Sometimes Frankie can be difficult, as you all know."

"Papa," Al addressed his father, "this isn't going to work the way we thought it would. I think we'll have to back up a little, to what Jacoby suggested, only instead of using the form letter, I'm asking all of you to go home, resolve the issue with your spouses, and then send me a confirming letter signed by each of you, alone. I'll have copies made for Jacoby, get his opinions and advice, and then we'll have another meeting. "That okay, Papa?"

Emil seemed pleased to have the meeting shortened, noting that Rosemary was still asleep. "That makes sense, Al. Everyone agree?" There were nods and murmured agreements all around. "Well then," the old man said, seeing his wife arouse herself, "Let's at least have one glass of wine to Mama," who perked up when she heard the suggestion. Glasses were filled, sports and other subjects were lightly discussed, and each went their own way.

CHAPTER TEN

As Lucy left her parents' home she began to worry about how Frankie would respond to Al's question about the cabin. She was pretty sure that he didn't really care about owning or having any interest in the cabin; she knew that he would just want to make sure that they got "their" share of the estate…preferably in cash. Trying to get into a more cheerful mood, she began reviewing the boy and girl names they had been considering; they had agreed not to have an ultra-sound sex determination. Since her parents' record was three and two, Lucy felt that it was a 50-50 chance no matter what. Thinking that they would have at least two children, she felt that the sex of the first one didn't matter. At the same time, she reflected on how strongly, in his macho way, Frankie had voiced his preference for a boy. Whether it was about the cabin or the baby, Lucy continued to be concerned about Frankie's attitude about both issues. She finally put all serious thoughts out of her mind, turned on some pleasant music on the car radio, and started thinking about what to prepare for dinner.

When Lucy had arrived home she automatically tripped the garage door opener, even though she had already decided to just park in the driveway because it was an easier walk into the house than going up the front steps. Frankie frequently put her car in the garage, and preferred doing so because it always irritated him if Lucy parked her car too close to his little sports car...which he never permitted her to drive.

Lucy was a bit surprised to see that his car was gone, but was not unduly alarmed because it was still only late afternoon, not quite dark. "Probably at his favorite sports bar cheering on the Suns' game with the rest of the bar flies," she said to herself as she entered the house through the garage door.

After slipping into a comfortable nightgown and a warm robe, Lucy busied herself preparing a salad to go with the left over lasagna from the night before last. Although she had stopped drinking anything alcoholic when she became pregnant, she cheerfully poured a glass of red wine for Frankie to have with his dinner. "That is, if he hasn't had too much to drink at the bar," she muttered half aloud. With the table set and dinner half ready, Lucy stretched herself out on the sofa and clicked on the TV, promptly falling asleep.

It was after six o'clock when Lucy awoke and immediately realized that Frankie was still not home. She fretted for a few minutes and then became fearful with the thought that an accident or something bad may have kept him from returning home. The pregnancy was enough to handle, she thought, "I don't need any more anxiety. Why hasn't he at least called me, even if he has some kind of problem?" She called his cell-phone number, but got only a recorded message. By seven o'clock Lucy was completely beside herself, and decided to call her brother Al, to see if he would know anything about where Frankie might be. Dinner was already over-cooked.

"Al, this is Lucy," she said with somewhat of a shaky voice.

"Well little sister, what gives rise to a call so soon? Did you and Frankie come to an agreement on the cabin question already?"

"I wish that that was the reason for my calling, Al, but I'm really worried about Frankie. He isn't home, and I have no idea where he might be. He hasn't called, and he should have been home hours ago. I called his cell phone number, but got no answer."

"Maybe he's at the folks. Have you called them?" Al asked.

Lucy said, "No, Al. I thought it was too early for that. They would worry."

"Relax," Al suggested in a quiet manner, "I'll call around. He's probably at a bar with some cronies and has had a few too many. Stay cool, kid, you don't have long to go you know. I'll get back to you as soon as I learn anything, but call me if he comes in, in the meantime."

Lucy did relax some; Al was right, she acknowledged. "Thanks, Al; I guess I'm more anxious because of having this baby. Hopefully, I'll call you, soon. She hung up the phone, but wrinkles in her forehead showed that the worry was still there.

To ease her mind she set up a tray-table in front of the TV and absent-mindedly ate her own dinner, such as it was. It was eight o'clock just then and the news was on. Lucy only half-heartedly listened to the reports, but she suddenly jerked wide awake when she heard a familiar name: "A Frank Salvo was found shot to death just a few hours ago on the outskirts of the city of Chandler. Preliminary information received stated that Mr. Salvo had connections with a crime mob and gamblers. Speculation is that it was likely a hit-man job because he was shot in the back of the head. In other news...Lucy fainted.

When she came to a minute later, she sat on the floor, stunned. The news was over, so she shut off the tube and began to cry. "Why? Why?" She repeated. "Frankie, Frankie, what did you do? Oh my baby! My baby!" she cried aloud as she held her bulging stomach.

CHAPTER ELEVEN

Days later, after their return from a three-week vacation in Los Angeles, Connie and Dick Horten were still playing catch-up with their laundromat business. Connie mostly at her little desk sorting out the remaining bills to be paid and Dick checking off the list of maintenance items he had taken care of. They had been fortunate in having Walter Agnew, the previous owner, fill in for them while they were gone, as he had done each of the last three years since he had sold them the business. He had admitted, jokingly, the first time he subbed for them, that it gave him the opportunity to see that the income would continue to be sufficient to cover the payments on the sales contract he held. Connie and Dick liked him and trusted him explicitly.

Walter had generated a list of maintenance items for Dick's use upon his return, mostly items that required more strength or energy than he possessed. When he turned the establishment back to Connie and Dick, he had assured them that everything had gone smoothly, but being conscientious he felt it necessary to check back with them just then. He walked in the front door with his usual jovial manner; "Hi again," he said to the pair," Happy to be back in the saddle?"

"Yes, thanks to you, Walter," Dick replied, "Everything is just fine and I really appreciate that work list you made out for me; I've knocked off about a third of the items so far."

"Have you emptied out all of the machines since you returned, Dick?" Walter asked. "I cleaned them out about ten days ago, but they should be fairly well loaded again."

"We've both been too busy up until now, but the traffic has been good, Walter, and we intend to clean them out just before we close up today. I found the receipts okay for the deposits that you made; they were right where you clipped them, on the desk calendar."

"I trust that it was alright for me to hire my big sixteen year-old grandson, Mark, to fill the water softener with salt. Those heavy bags are just too much for me anymore. I also had him come in every Saturday morning to help clean up the place. I paid him in cash, of course, and put a chit in the petty cash box for what I paid him."

"Of course, Walter; that was just fine. I remember meeting him last year; a nice boy. As long as you're here, if you have the time, how about helping me empty the machines now. I'd really like to Connie leave early, she has her own car and could take the coins home and wrap them while our dinner would be defrosting. Then I could continue working the list."

From her desk, Connie said, "I heard that and I'm all in favor of the idea."

"Be glad to, Dick; Martha's playing bridge and told me not to rush home when I told her that I planned to stop by the laundromat. Let's get to it."

The two men cleaned out the machines, put the bags of coins in Connie's car, and she closed up her desk and left for home with her treasure.

Connie looked forward eagerly to separating, counting, and wrapping the coins. It was always a job that gave her a little kick because it made her feel as elated as when she won money at the casino. She slipped into a comfortable at-home dress, fixed herself a cup of coffee, and then carefully spread all of the coins out on a card table, with a pile of nickel, dime, and quarter wrappers on a TV tray next to her. She still watched for silver coins, even though she knew that it was unlikely that she would find any; collectors had all of the silver coins nowadays.

Her long black hair drifted over her eyes, and as she paused to brush it away, her thoughts drifted back to the cabin problem as she continued to separate the coins into their respective piles, almost unconsciously. "Maybe we shouldn't sign off on the cabin," she thought, "we may tire of traveling some day, and summer weekends up in the cool country would be pretty nice." She closed her big brown eyes and looked up, as though imagining the cabin amongst the tall green pines. She decided to discuss her idea with Dick when he came home, and hoped that he would be agreeable. They surely would not need the money for her share of the estate. "If nothing else," she thought, "maybe we could be co-owners with one of the others. Al and Jean would be great; their boys could help maintain the place." The more she thought about it, the more she became convinced that she had resolved the question, at least in her own mind.

Her reverie was broken by the telephone ring, startling her; she almost knocked the coins off of the table. So that it would be handy, Connie had put the portable phone on the TV tray. She lifted the receiver; it was Al.

"Hi Sis, hope I haven't caught you at a bad time."

"Not at all, big brother," Connie said cheerfully. "Just doing my favorite thing, which you know is counting the coin take from the Laundromat. What's up?"

"I hate to spoil your fun, kiddo, but we just lost our brother-in-law."

Connie paled, "What? How?" She almost shouted, knowing that it had to be Frank. "Did he crash his car? Tell me! Tell me!" She was flushed, and in a sweat immediately.

"Whoa, slow down kid, or you'll have a heart attack. We don't need any more bad news. We don't have all of the details yet, but apparently Frankie must have made enemies of some bad people. He was shot right behind his favorite bar, and the little that we know indicates that he was acquainted with the shooter and the man that was with him." Before Al could say any more, Connie exploded.

"Shot! Oh my God! Poor Lucy...what is she going to do? She is due any time now. Why? Why?" She put the phone down, unable to talk anymore. Al understood and quietly hung up. There was nothing more to be said, but it was obvious to him that it would be concern for Lucy that would affect the whole family.

CHAPTER TWELVE

Al sat in his car, parked in his parent's driveway. He had cracked the driver's window before shutting off the engine; he took some deep breaths before going in the house to tell them the bad news about Frankie. He leaned forward over the steering wheel, and rubbed both hands over his balding head. How could he possibly tell them about Frankie? It wasn't just the fact that he was dead, but it was how he died that made his task so much more difficult. Then it dawned on him that they may have already caught the news from a television or radio broadcast. He was torn as to just what he should do, but finally roused himself, left the car, and wearily climbed the front steps to the door. Emil was opening the door at that moment.

"What's wrong, Al?" the father said, "I saw you pull up awhile ago, and waited for you to come in. You don't look very happy; are you okay?"

"Not really, Papa. This is not a good time for the DiBiasi family. Let's go sit down somewhere with Mama. Is she alright?"

Emil hesitated, wanting to know right away what was wrong, but he conceded to his son's wishes. "Of course, Al, let's go into the kitchen. Mama's fine, she's in there fixing lunch. She'd be happy if you could join us." He led the way, alerting his wife of Al's arrival, "Look, Mama, Al's here; might join us for lunch."

Rosemary perked up, as she always does when any member of the family visits; she was a typical Italian mother; she loved them all, no matter what. She draped her dishtowel on the counter, gently put down the cup she had been drying, and greeted her son with a kiss on the cheek. "Al, How nice to see you." She embraced him, letting the strength of his body steady her own slender figure. Slowly re-moving herself from his arms, she asked, "Can you stay for lunch?" Then she perceived Al's serious mood, and said, "You look worried, son, are you okay? Or is there something else the matter? Is Jean alright?" The old lady was getting herself distraught.

Al nodded, and said, "No, no, Mama, Jean and I are both just fine, but I do have some troubling news. Let's sit here at the table," which is where the family members usually convened. The kitchen was where Mama loved to have her family, where she could serve them her favorite treats...apple pie or cinnamon cookies. They took seats at the sides of the square table, but it bothered Al that his parents should be showing their anxiety over whatever they thought he had to tell them. It was enough for them just to be coping with all of the effects of their advancing ages. He was worried about any impact on their health that might result from hearing the bad news.

It was a difficult task, but Al chose his words carefully, watching their reactions with considerable apprehension. Mama let out several small whimpers as the event was described to them; Papa moved his chair close to her and she leaned her head on his shoulder. Neither could collect themselves enough to verbally express their feelings, yet in a way, they acted as though they were not surprised.

After a few moments Papa said, "Do the police have any clues as to who might have shot Frankie, or why it was done? It seems, from what you have told us, that Frankie was in the bar and walked out the back door with two men, and one of them shot him. You would think that some customer, a waitress, or the bartender would be able to identify one or both of the two men, or at least give the police some kind of description."

Al had given his message rather briefly, trying to spare his parents the despair he knew they would feel if the details of the murder were described, but he felt that he had to respond to Papa's question. "I'm afraid that as of right now, Papa, the police have made no progress in solving the crime. There is only speculation that it was done because of Frankie's unpaid gambling debts. The police have pretty well ruled out any bad drug deal. Of course the media has jumped in the fray and added to the confusion over the cause. I'll try to keep you informed, but I doubt if I'll be able to tell you much more than you can get from the news reports."

Al decided that he should leave his parents to cope with the news in their own way. He had been as gentle as he could be in relating the sad event. "What more could I have said?" he questioned himself, and rose from his chair. He kissed his mother on the forehead and gave his father a pat on the shoulder. "I'll call you later," he said, and left quietly.

After Al left, Emil told his wife, "You were right, Mama, Frankie was into something illegal, or criminal. I honestly can't believe that it was over gambling debts; it had to be something else. I wouldn't be surprised if it was by a jealous husband, whose wife Frankie got too chummy with. Maybe it had something to do with the kind of work he did. You always felt that there was some reason he never said much about his job."

Mama finally let loose, "Oh my God! Lucy! Lucy! What will she do now? Oh, Papa, what should we do?" Emil was silent, unable to suggest anything. Questions about the cabin no longer seemed important.

CHAPTER THIRTEEN

Although Frankie was really anti-religious, Lucy was compelled, because of her own strict Roman Catholic background, to have a normal funeral service for him, and was happy to have Al make the arrangements for it. The parish priest, Father O'Brian, knew Lucy very well, but had only met Frankie a few times, at weddings of family members and friends; he was aware of Frankie's negative attitude toward the church, but enjoyed a very good relationship with all other members of the DiBiasi family. When Al asked him to officiate at the service, he asked Al to give him some personal information about Frankie, in order to bring in some comments that would lend the service a bit of the personal reflection of the man. Al could only say that Frankie was a good husband to Lucy and provided well for her. Beyond that, Al was unable to give the priest much to work with for the service. He did tell Father O'Brian that Frankie had not connected well with the family since he married Lucy four years ago. "He must have had some drinking friends though, Father, because we all knew that he spent a lot of time at a sports bar in Chandler. Maybe he was a good sports fan. We never did know, exactly, what he did for a living; Lucy said that he worked for a contractor of some kind and that he had a lot of free time."

The priest thanked Al for the limited information, but at the same time wondered what he could say about a man that most likely was more aligned with the devil than with God, and about whom he knew very little.

There were very few people in attendance at the service, including a few that none of the family members recognized. There were particularly, two men who stood at the back of the church that seemed to be just curious, with no real interest in the proceeding. They were not attired in a fashion generally seen at funeral services.

Lucy had moved laboriously into a front row seat, and sat there silently throughout the service, her head bowed, seemingly not in prayer, but in muted grief and confusion. She could not bring an iota of understanding into her mind of what had happened, or why.

Al and Jean sat on either side of her for moral support. Emil and Rosemary DiBiasi were ushered into the same pew and were seated next to Al. The rest of the family took seats behind them in the little side chapel often used for small parties. Jean had always felt like a big sister to Lucy, and they had grown quite close after Lucy became pregnant. Having had two children of her own, Jean had been able to offer Lucy helpful advice over the last eight and a half months, and now suffered the pain Lucy was enduring over the loss of her husband. Some in the family felt only mock sorrow over Frankie's passing, because he had really never ingratiated himself with the whole family, or any part of it, for that matter.

The service was brief; no one stepped forward to pay a personal tribute, and everyone almost felt sorry for Father O'Brian, who tried to fill the void by emphasizing the need of support for the wife of the decease and encouraging prayers for her and her unborn child. He made no mention of Frankie's non-religious belief or the manner in which he had died, lamenting only about how young he was to have passed on.

There was not going to be a burial; Al had taken charge of the affair and had convinced Lucy that a cremation was best, thus eliminating the historical graveside mourning. He had also selected and ordered an appropriate urn for the ashes, having lost the argument with Lucy over just burying a simple container with the ashes.

The two unidentified men exited moments before the service was over, but both Al and Jeremy had noticed them leave. As the group started to depart after the service, Jerry stopped Al and quietly asked, "Did you see two rough looking men at the back of the church?"

Al replied, "Yeah, I saw them, just for a second before they started to leave. They were there for some reason, I'm sure, and from the looks of them they probably know more than we do about Frankie's murder. It was pretty obvious to me that they were more interested in who was here, rather than in the service. They had to have known Frankie. Don't say anything to Lucy or Mama and Papa; no sense in giving them anything more to worry about. I don't believe that they were at all aware of the presence of those two characters. Let's keep this between ourselves until we find out more about those guys. We can do some sleuthing on our own. If there is a connection with Frankie, Lucy could be in danger. She may have something that they want, or has some information they would like to have. I think that it might be wise for you and I to check up on her more often; why don't you call her sometime every morning and I'll call every afternoon, at least until we feel confident that she is not in any danger."

"That makes sense, Al. I know Frankie's favorite sports bar, it's on Ray road in Chandler. He hung out there a lot. I'll sit at the bar and take my time with some draft beer and try to pick up on anything the bar flies might be talking about. I'm sure that Frankie's murder has to be big news there. I'll call you if I get lucky. One thing we know: the police have already established that it wasn't a robbery."

Al nodded in agreement and the two of them joined the exiting group, which moved very quietly out of the church and slowly into their individual autos. It was truly a somber event, and everyone was glad that it was over.

CHAPTER FOURTEEN

The last customer to come in, just a minute before Gus was to close up the pharmacy, was one of the "select" customers; one who received his "prescription" with little comment and paid in cash. Gus greeted him with apprehension because he was the last of his irregulars to be informed that Gus was discontinuing the special service.

"Glad you came in, Shorty; I've been expecting you, but this is Tuesday; you usually come by early on Saturday mornings. Everything all right?"

"Oh, I'm fine, Gus, but I'm having trouble with my girl friend. Damn! Why do women always cause trouble? Now she thinks that she needs a cocaine hit twice a day; I can't afford that; I told her so. Now she is threatening to walk the streets to pay for more crack. I'm about to skip out; screw it, I can't hack it…unless you can help me out Gus, and cut the price," he said in almost a pleading voice.

"I'm sorry about that, Shorty, but I won't be in a position to accommodate you anymore, even for your normal needs. I'm shutting down; I just can't risk it anymore; it's affecting my health."

"Oh bullshit, Gus, you're as healthy as you have ever been. There must be some other reason. Christ! Don't tell me you're not making enough money off your special customers to justify the risk. You've got to be clearing at least an extra five grand a month."

"I won't lie to you, Shorty; we've done business together for too many years, but I've got problems at home. Although she doesn't know about my sideline, I think that she has to be wondering what's wrong with me. Our sex life is non-existent, which is my fault, and I'm afraid she may be looking elsewhere. Haven't you noticed my tic? And it's getting worse. I've got to do something; maybe even sell out."

"So do you think you could arrange something for me with another pharmacy? You owe me Gus, I've been a good customer, as you just said." A bit of anger in his voice.

Gus squirmed a bit as he stood behind the white counter; he had seen Shorty when he was angry before, or in need of a fix; he could be difficult. He had to give a reply. I'm not sure what I can do; most all of the pharmacists that I know work in small stores, and the big chains are out of the question. The ones I know play the game pretty straight, but I'll see what I can do." He gave Shorty his usual purchase, put the cash in his white jacket pocket and walked Shorty to the door.

Shorty settled himself a little and said, "I'm sorry about that tic, Gus, but what about all of your other special customers, where are they going to be taken care of? I know some of them and I know that they felt safe buying from you; never had to worry about getting contaminated goods."

Gus had his hand on the door handle, anxious to have Shorty leave when the phone rang; Shorty shrugged his shoulders, knowing Gus had to answer the phone, and left with a nod as Gus closed the door after him. He hurried back to the counter and answered "DiBiasi Pharmacy," even though he expected the call to be from Elaine. It wasn't.

"Gus, this is Tim Mahoney from the Westwind Hospital; are you busy or do you have a minute to talk?"

"I was just closing up, plenty of time to talk. Nice to hear from you again, Tim; any special problem?"

"Everything is going just fine at the hospital, Gus, but not for me. That's why I am calling you. My wife Julie got a big surprise from back home in Blue Springs; she has just inherited a small strip shopping center there; you may remember, that is where she grew up. Anyway, there is a pharmacy in that center and she wants us to go back there; I could take over the pharmacy and she would be back with some of her family"

"Don't tell me," Gus said, "that you are going to leave that cushy hospital job and move to Blue Springs in Kansas! I thought you loved Arizona and the nice warm weather, where you can swim and play golf all year round. Well if you go, I'll bet that you will eventually come back here. Anyway, what does that have to do with me, Tim?"

"I have already given my notice here, Gus, and the management has asked me to recommend a replacement for me. I took the liberty of submitting your name. I told them, of course, that it would be iffy because you have your own store."

"Gosh, Tim; that was nice of you to suggest me, but I don't know. This is a big surprise, something I would have to give serious thought to, talk to Elaine about it, and see what I could do about my own store."

"I know, the whole thing has been a surprise for me too. I know that you have had a successful business where you are, but think, Gus, you wouldn't have to worry about getting business, and as an employee of a great hospital you will have the best medical coverage, a pension plan, and a profit-sharing program, all with regular hours. It has been a wonderful career for me here for the last twelve years; I really hate to leave, but Julie has twisted my arm. Maybe I'll get to like it there, small town and all. What do you think? Is it possible?"

"How soon do you need my answer? I'll talk to Elaine, naturally, but more importantly, I have to decide what and how I can sell, close, or get someone to manage this place. I need at least a week, but I must say, Tim, the more I think about it, the more intriguing it sounds."

"Okay; we don't have to leave for Blue Springs until the end of April, so we have three weeks to firm up my replacement. If you agree, and can arrange everything, I will feel that I've done something good for the hospital and for you, as a good friend. Should it all work out, the four of us could celebrate with a bon voyage dinner, my treat. Call me as soon as you can, one way or another, so I'll know what to tell the management. No problem with them approving you, I guarantee it. Say hello to Elaine."

Tim hung up and Gus's brain was in a whirl. He first thought about what it would be like to give up his independence, yet he could visualize how relaxed he might be, with less business pressure, a clean cut-off from Shorty and his ilk. "Maybe my tic will disappear completely," he thought, "and maybe I will have more energy and be a new man with Elaine." He drove home feeling very upbeat, and when he entered the front door he greeted Elaine with an unusually sexy kiss. "Fix me a scotch and water tonight, kiddo," he ordered in a polite but strong tone, "I've got some interesting news that may give us a new lease on life, and a happier one." He seemed to glow with enthusiasm that Elaine hadn't seen for a long time.

Elaine's eyes widened with the surprising energy her husband was showing. She fixed Gus his scotch and water and one for herself. Handing it to him, she said, "Here you are my man; whatever change you're talking about, I'm for it."

CHAPTER FIFTEEN

"I know, I know," Jake Jacoby replied to a caller on his phone, obviously irritated, "But I think that we should cool it for awhile. Right now I'm not concerned about our activity up north; my concern is making sure that you and I and Santos are clear of any indication that we had an involvement with Frankie's death. So far as we know, the police have leaned toward his being eliminated by hit men because he couldn't repay his gambling I.O.U.'s. The way Santos did it, in the back of the head, adds credibility to their conclusion. Actually, that could have happened to him anyway if we hadn't shut his mouth first. I know that he had a lot of chits outstanding, all because he couldn't stay away from the craps tables. I don't think that any of Frankie's family is going to go up to the cabin until it warms up, the snow melts, the ski season is over, and the country club opens up the dining room, or at least the golf course is open for play. We have lots of time, probably at least four or five more weeks before checking on the cabin to see if we left anything there that could be traced to any of us. Frankly, I'm not sure that we really need or should go up there; it might not be the smartest thing to do right now. I'll have to give it some more thought."

On the other end of the line, Ziggy Rios shrugged his shoulders and answered back, "You're calling the shots, Mr. J., whatever you say, but what about Frankie's wife? We really don't know if she has a clue about Frankie's tie with us, or whether she knows our names, or anything. If we knew more about what she knows about our operation, it may help us decide what we should do about her...if anything. Right now she's carrying a watermelon, but she can still talk. Her mouth could give us trouble, just like Frankie's almost did."

"As of now," Jake replied, "she is grieving and concerned about having her baby, her financial affairs, and her parents. The few times that I was with Mr. & Mrs. DiBiasi and some of the family, Frankie wasn't even there, and his wife hardly knew me. I doubt if she ever thought that we were connected in any way. It would surprise me if even the police are bothering her much; after all, she is the victim's wife, not a suspect in the murder. It probably didn't take long for the cops to realize that she had nothing to do with the shooting. I don't believe that Frankie had any million-dollar life insurance policy, for a motive, and he was about to become a father. That's the only thing that bothers me about axing him. To play it safe, though, you and Santos put a bug in her house and set up a monitoring unit to tape her in and out calls. Don't do any search work; we don't want to leave signs that someone had been in the house. Let me know when it's done."

"Okay, Mr. J., we'll probably have it set up tomorrow or the next day. My guess is that she will be staying at her folks for a while, or with one of her brothers. If that is the case, we won't get much from bugging her place; all we'll get will be incoming calls. That's a chance I guess we'll just have to take. In any event, I agree with you in having it done. She might stay away for just one or two days, which might make it easier for Santos and me to install the bug. I'll call you when everything is in place. With Frankie gone though, how are we going to carry on with our regular business? He had a lot of contacts and handled most of the traffic in New Mexico and Nevada. We'll have to notify those people as to his replacement, if you take on another man. I can handle my area and his for a little while, but I'll be chasing my tail after a month or so. If you want me to, I have a few friends in a related business, and I would bet that at least one of them would be happy to give up being a retailer and would like to get in on the wholesale side of the business. Most of them know who we are. Let me know what you decide, and I'll take it from there." Ziggy then hung up.

Jacoby sat quietly in his executive chair, slowly unwrapping a fresh cigar, and pondered over the situation. He lit the cigar with his silver lighter almost unconsciously, with the flame over burning the butt of the cigar before he realized what he was doing. He wondered what the devil he could do about Lucy Salvo if it turned out that she knew much about how Frankie made a living. He wasn't sure that he could have her quieted in any way. Christ! If she weren't pregnant if would be different.

Everything had been going along very nicely for a long time, no problems, now he had some concerns about the future of his operation. Frankie had been a good soldier, doing what he was told to do, most of the time. When he was sober he could do whatever was necessary. The problem, which he had not lived to regret, was that when he had too much to drink he developed a loose tongue. Ziggy had overheard him in the bar talking about two bodies buried "up near Flagstaff." He hadn't mentioned Pinewood or Munds Park, fortunately. Nor did he say anything about the DiBiasi cabin. Jacoby puffed slowly on his cigar, but began to wonder if he needed to replace the loss of one of his group. "Damn!" he thought, "drinking is one thing, but why the hell couldn't he have kept his mouth shut!" He knew that Santos was not very happy about having to take care of the problem; he and Frankie had done a lot of jobs together. "Oh, what the hell," Jacoby uttered out loud, "It had to be done."

CHAPTER SIXTEEN

Hugo Santos brought two steins of draft beer to the corner table at the Z-Bar in Chandler and sat down with a resounding thud, his 240 pounds causing the wood chair to creak loudly. Other customers in the vicinity looked around because they thought that the chair was broken. He handed his partner, Ziggy Rios, one of the beers with a look of displeasure.

"Damn it, Ziggy, why did you tell Mr. J. that we would bug Frankie's house today? I thought that we could goof off this weekend, like we planned, go to the track and play the horses. I don't see that putting a bug in Frankie's house will do us any good; what the hell could his wife know that would hurt us anyhow? Besides that, how do we know that she will even be there; she could be staying at her folks place now that Frankie is gone. Or she could be at the home of one of her brothers or at her sisters, and we know that she might be delivering that baby any time now and will be in the hospital for a while. Knowing Frankie, I can't see him telling his wife anything about our business. He drank too much, but he wasn't stupid; he just had a big mouth when he drank. I think it's a waste of time."

"Calm down Santos, you're getting worked up over nothing; remember that I told him that we would <u>probably</u> do it tomorrow or the next day; we don't have to do it tonight. Mr. J. thinks that we might learn something from bugging Frankie's house, and what might be there that could connect us to Frankie, but we can decide ourselves when we want to do it. Actually, Santos, I think that Jacoby is more worried about anything popping up that might tie <u>him</u> to Frankie, than to us. I think that he ought to have us scout around the cabin first, especially since we used the cabin not too long ago. I didn't want to question Jacoby, but I agree with you; bugging the house is going to be a waste of time. Another thing, I don't know what he thought we might learn by going to Frankie's funeral; to me it was a mistake because someone there probably saw us and could identify us later, for one reason or another. All we could tell him anyway was that it looked like just the family was there, and I didn't hear any sobbing, not even from the widow. She had that big tummy with Frankie's baby, but she is still a pretty good looking chick. Just between you and me, I am beginning to wonder if Jacoby is slipping; he's not the same dynamo he was when we hooked up with him, and right now he is wondering whether to take on someone to replace Frankie and also how to keep the operation running. He seems to have more trouble making decisions lately; I think maybe he has smoked too many cigars. He's polluted his brain."

Santos slugged down half of his beer in one gulp, then wiped his mouth with the back of his hand. "I know he is calling the shots, but I guess I'm just a bit wary of Jacoby since I silenced Frankie for him. I still haven't seen the bonus he promised me for doing the job. He's always paid us as he promised, but I think he likes to string us along for a while first. Either that, or as you say, he doesn't have all of his cylinders working.

"Oh, hell, forget what I've said; so what's your plan?"

"Look, I've got six of the bugs, that ought to be enough for that small house, and I've got the tapes, and the recorder. Once we get in the house it should only take a minute or so to place the bugs. You've seen her place, an older home with windows that have the old snap locks. A piece of cake. I'll call her number and if there's no answer she is sure to be at one of her family's places. And unless she had one installed recently, I know that Frankie didn't have a security system, even though the house is not in the best neighborhood. After we get the bugs placed, I can check the reception of the recorder before we even get out of the door. I'm thinking that we can do it early this evening, or even later, so we can still go to the track this afternoon. The track doesn't open until twelve, and the races don't start until one. We'll have plenty of time to get there, have lunch, and be ready for some betting when the windows open."

"Sounds okay, but what if she's home, then what?"

"You know, on second thought, maybe we should skip it tonight," Rios answered. "She's Catholic, right? So Sunday morning is probably a lot safer for us; she will be in church, unless she is somewhere delivering her baby. In either case, I think that early tomorrow morning will be the best time for the job. Drink up your beer, partner; I'll buy another, then we can go to the track right now."

"Now you're talking," Santos laughed. "Almost makes me happy that some people are religious." They both laughed and clinked glasses as they finished their beer and Ziggy hailed the waitress over to order another round.

CHAPTER SEVENTEEN

The winter had been fairly mild south of Flagstaff, although the San Francisco Peaks had received ample snow to keep the skiers jumping happily over the moguls. The Snow Bowl lift chairs had seen a steady stream of patrons every weekend since December, and the weekday traffic was the best in three years. The operators were very happy.

Down in Munds Park, nineteen miles south, preparations were getting underway to handle the summer residents who would soon be moving into their cabins, condos, townhouses, and manufactured single and double-wide homes in Pinewood, the major development in Munds Park. Across I-17, activity was stirring in the motor home and trailer park area...Pinewood's cousin facility.

The woodpiles near the houses and cabins owned by year-'round residents were shrinking, but snow was still piled on each side of the driveways and walkways. Pet dogs were slowly getting a bit more romping room.

As temperatures began to ease, the Pinewood Sanitary District, which manages the huge processing plant, began to conduct more sewer pipeline connections and repairs in order to keep the sewage flowing for the area residences and businesses as the summer folks moved in. This meant, of course, that some crews would be working on the lines and manholes, repairing joints and leaks.

The terrain around the DiBiasi cabin was extremely rocky; the builder had struggled to get through the rocks when the cabin was built, and the Sanitary District was forced to cross into adjacent property when laying the sewer pipe. There were no clear areas to plant bushes, flowers, or other plants. Dirt had to be brought in and laid atop the rocks in order to have any landscaping at all. What made the area attractive was that the cabin sat on the high side of W. Oak, with the road dropping down on each side, thus providing great drainage, especially when the snow would be melting. It was also very close to the edge of the Coconino National Forest...which even in the daytime looked mysterious.

Frankie and his associates had scouted the area years ago, and they had held some meetings at the DiBiasi cabin, which was unknown to the family. The group felt safe, believing that their use of the cabin and the forest would never be known to anyone else, and for a time that was true. After today, that would change.

The two workers from the Sanitary District were up to their ankles in mud, just to the east of the DiBiasi cabin, at one of the rare spots in the area free from immovable rocks. Engrossed in trying to reconnect a pipe joint, they were suddenly aware of two eyes peering at them from about twenty feet away. As they looked up, the eyes moved quickly toward the fringe of the Coconino forest, leaving the workers staring at the hind end of a coyote.

"Well, Bert, Henry said to his partner, "I guess he doesn't want our company."

"No meal here, either, but I'm glad that it wasn't a bear," Bert replied.

Henry paused in his work and said, "Now that you've mentioned food, I think I'm ready for some." He laid his big wrench on a flat rock as he suggested, "Let's have lunch. I know it's a bit early, but I'm hungry."

Bert took off his gloves and started to extract himself from the mud. "I'm ready too, pal. Let's find a log in the woods to park on. It should be a bit dry in there, and maybe we'll see our little coyote friend again."

The two men tramped the fifty yards or so into the fringe of the woods, stomping the mud off of their boots against old tree stumps on their way. They passed by several fallen pine trees as they moved further into the forest, but rejected them because of the wet bark, finally settling on a huge boulder that provided a fairly dry flat area. Opening up their lunch boxes, they sat quietly munching their thick sandwiches and watched a few nut-hunting squirrels scampering from one area to another. The men enjoyed their antics and starting throwing some of their sandwich bread toward them.

One of the squirrels chased after a tidbit that had fallen into a small crevice, then used his paws to pull up what appeared to be a small twig. Bert saw the action and looked quizzically at the twig, thinking that it had an odd color. He put his half-eaten sandwich back in his lunch box and moved toward the small crevice, causing the squirrel to scat. He reached down and grasped what he now thought to be a bone, examined it, and then took it over to Henry. "Look at this," he said, "It has to be a bone, probably dropped by a coyote, but it is an odd shape. What do you think, Hank?"

"I've done a lot of hunting in this forest over the years, Bert, and I have skinned a lot of big and small game, but that bone doesn't look like anything that I've seen. Let's have a look-see at that area where you got the bone. Maybe there are more bones there that will help us determine what kind of creature was buried there, or if it was just some stray coyote leftovers."

Hank kicked the ground around where the squirrel had been digging, and very quickly turned to Bert with an almost fearful look on his face. "Better get on your cell phone, Bert, and put in a call to the sheriff's office. This looks like some child or small person has been buried here." He held up another bone to his partner, who had already started to run to their truck for the phone.

Several sheriff's deputies showed up within minutes, examined the area where the bones were found and decided that they were not prepared to cope with what appeared to be at least the remains of one, if not two, human bodies. A call was made to Flagstaff with the report of the findings, and the deputies were merely told to secure the area, and that help would be provided to assist them, either by others from the Sheriff's office, the Phoenix police, or possibly even the FBI.

The following day, both the Phoenix Arizona Republic and the Flagstaff Papers reported that the fairly decomposed bodies of two children had been uncovered near the edge of the Coconino forest in Munds Park. The ages and identities of the victims had not been established, but the guess was that they were both females in their early teens.

CHAPTER EIGHTEEN

Al Dibiasi was reading the morning paper while enjoying his coffee when he nearly dropped them both. "My God Jean! You won't believe this."

Jean replied, almost absent mindedly as she continued to read herself, "What?"

It was as if he had not heard her; he just went on reading, until Jean in an exasperating reaction, said, "What? What?" That finally got his attention, and he turned his head toward her, and reported on the article he had been reading.

"Listen to this," he said, "it's incredible. Two workers from the Sanitary District discovered the remains of two teenage girls in the forest while working on one of their lines, and from the how they described the area, it is not very far from the family cabin. Wow!"

Jean dropped her newspaper, was startled, and said, "I can't believe that! The only crime that I can ever remember in all of Pinewood, or all of Munds Park for that matter, was one or two vandalisms over the last twenty years. Murders? It can't be! Nothing like any violent crime has ever occurred there that I know of, including the RV park. Have they identified the girls?"

"Not yet," Al replied. Apparently they had been there a number of months; the bodies were pretty well deteriorated; they were only able to recover bones and some clothing, all in fairly good condition, and which are being analyzed in the hope it will lead them to the murderer or murderers, and why they were killed. They are speculating at this point, of course, but someone was quoted anonymously in the paper that the bodies had not been there more than six months. The sheriff is also quoted as saying that if they had been buried just one foot deeper, they would have never been found." Al added his own opinion on that point, "I have to agree with that statement, because it isn't likely that there will ever be any excavating or large construction work in a national forest, at least not in our lifetime. That's most probably what the murderer thought. It had to be purely a matter of luck to have had two PSD workers taking a lunch break, as the paper said, and be right at that spot. I'll bet the odds against that happening are probably a million to one to have had that happen."

Jean put down her paper and looked sorrowfully toward Al. "I shudder to think about their parents," she voiced, "what must they be going through if they don't know where their daughters are. Wouldn't it be horrible if it turns out that they were sisters? My Lord! Who could do such a thing," she asked rhetorically.

"That would be terrible, or if they were even related, Jean, but I doubt it; however it would be plausible that they may have known each other. They may have just been friends playing in the woods when it happened; one of those wrong-place, wrong-time situations. That is going to shake up all of the local communities, all the way to Flagstaff, including Kachina Village, Mountainaire, and even the new development, Foxboro…and it won't be good publicity for any of them. One thing that I am pretty sure about, though, is that it is unlikely that the girls were from anywhere nearby. If any girls from Munds Park had run away, or had been missing, I'm sure that it would have been a major story in the Pinewood News. That little paper would have reported it if any girls were missing from any of the local communities, even from Flagstaff. They had to be from someplace else."

Still sitting with the newspaper on her lap, somewhat in shock, Jean's eyes reflected her alarm as she reflected on the gruesome event. "Al."

Her husband, who had continued to read, absent mindedly responded, "What?"

Jean sat straight up and said again, "Al," then she paused, as if unsure of what she wanted to say. "Listen to me." Al obediently put down his paper and Jean addressed him again. "Do you think that there might be a connection between the murder of those two girls and Frankie, or the way and why he was killed? I know it sounds crazy, but the thought just popped into my head; the whole thing just seems all too unreal to be true; it's boggling my brain."

"I can't see that as a possibility, Jean, after all he was killed in Chandler, that's a long way from Munds Park. I don't know how you could come up with such a crazy thought. My bet would be that those girls were hiking and as I said, they were in the wrong spot at the wrong time; they were likely raped and then killed by some homeless bums camping in the forest. Just bad luck. I hope that they get the bastards before there are any more victims."

Jean frowned, "That's all Mama and Papa need. First Frankie and Lucy's pregnancy, and now murders in Pinewood. Let's hope that all this unpleasantness doesn't bring on a heart attack for either one of them. This has got to be scary for them; to think that there were murders that close to their cabin. Wow."

CHAPTER NINETEEN

Lawyer Jake Jacoby sat uneasily in his executive chair, twisting a still unwrapped cigar around in his left hand, while he tapped the desktop nervously with the ring on his right hand. Ziggy and Santos sat back on their conference chairs; no one was smiling. With obvious reluctance, Ziggy broke the silence, "Well Mr. J. now what?"

"It's as plain as the scar on your neck, Ziggy; we've got to shut down. No more girls from Mexico, at least for a while...until we see how this plays out. Look, according to the papers, the police have no leads on Frankie's murder, and they are just speculating about the two girls. They haven't yet discovered that they both had Herpes and were HIV positive. If we had sold them and then and our customers found out how sick they were it would have killed our business, or one of them would have killed us if they had become infected. Our customers are not all Gentlemen Jim's. Even worse, if they had sought treatment somewhere they could have furnished a path right back to this office. I offered a hundred bucks each and a trip back to Mexico, but they refused; they didn't want to go back. Even though they didn't speak much English, as you know, they still understood it quite well. In the short time they were here, they got to acting pretty cocky, and I felt that they might have been planning to leave us. Maybe they had somehow connected with a Van Buren pimp who offered them a nice furnished apartment; that usually suckers them in. The real clincher was when the little one patted her stomach and smiled at her friend. That would have been all we needed: a mother and baby with HIV and Herpes. Damn those two assholes in Sonora; they should never have sent them up here in the first place. It was unfortunate, but they had to go. You earned your bonus, Santos; it was just a crazy coincidence that caused them to find the bodies. When we open up for business again, which I feel sure we will, we won't deal with Gonzales or Garcia again, for damn sure. They were ordered to check every girl for any kind of sexual disease."

"What about money Mr. J?" Santos broke in. "I'm pretty low on cash right now, and I've got to have enough dough to get me by until you start up the operation again. I thought maybe I should go stay with my older sister is Frisco. She's a widow, but she has a pretty good pension check coming in every month. I can sponge off her for a while; do odd jobs around the house to help pay my room and board. Actually, she might be very glad to have me there, as security. I don't think she will say no because I am her only living relative now. Don't think I told you, Mr. J., I got rid of the gun that took care of Frankie, don't worry about that, but I could use my bonus for that job and a bit more cash until you call us back."

Jake shot back, alarmed about how the gun was disposed of. "You didn't sell it, did you? Hell, that's no guarantee that it won't surface and get traced back to you."

"Relax boss," Santos assured him, "it's in the deep six, middle of Lake Odell. That's pure mud on the bottom; the gun will sink out of sight, and draining that little lake would be a waste of time. That rod is gone for good."

"Okay, Jake said, "good work. I want you to leave tomorrow. Stop by my place in the morning; I'll have enough cash to last you quite awhile, including your bonus. That's a lucky break, having your sister's place available."

Santos seemed relieved. "I'm leaving now then, boss, I've got some packing to do and some papers to get rid of. I'll call you when I check in at my sister's, and I'll give you her phone number so you can call me when you start up again." He left hurriedly after shaking hands with Jake and Ziggy.

"Now Ziggy," Jacoby said, "you've got to get on the horn to Mexico and stop any "deliveries" right away; then call our "distributors" in California, Nevada, and New Mexico. I'll call Frankie's customers here in the Phoenix area, and explain to them that it is just a temporary situation brought about by a clamp down by the immigration authorities, and that we expect business as usual very shortly. Use our usual code words; don't answer any questions or try to explain anything. Just say that you're following orders. You'll never get off the phone if you try to explain too much, and you sure as hell can't tell them the real reason for the interruption. Get started right now. I gave Sandy the day off, so use her phone. I have some other things to do." He left with a hand wave. "I'll call you later at your place."

Ziggy moved to the secretary's desk, sat there for a moment; did not lift the phone. He had a sinking feeling in the pit of his stomach; he knew that it might be sometime before he would be able to make the kind of money he had been making with Jacoby. He started thinking about what he could do for income; Jacoby had probably already written him off. He had to start thinking of himself. He finally rose to his feet and said to no one: "The hell with it! I didn't kill anyone; I only helped bury two useless girls that Santos and Frankie killed. I'm outta here!" He grabbed his coat and hat and was out the door, slamming it behind him.

Jake finally unwrapped and lit his fresh cigar as he walked to his car, considering whether he should head to the bank for cash, or not. "Damn!" he muttered out loud, "just when things were going well." As he calmed down and puffed on his cigar, he realized that to give the appearance that all is well he probably should call on the DiBiasi's; he thought too, that they may have been interviewed by the police, either as the in-laws of Frankie Salvo or as owners of a cabin near where the remains of the two girls had been found. He had to act as though everything was normal, which wouldn't be easy.

He drove there slowly, thinking about his former legal practice. Why couldn't he have been more successful? How could he have been dumb enough to let Frankie Salvo convince him that Mexican girls could make him rich? Then he remembered that at that time Julie had left him, and the thought of having a selection of young girls to satisfy his lust was inviting. Being 49 at that time, and with his income down, he had no ambition to find pleasure elsewhere. He bought into the deal. Jake snapped out of his muse as he pulled into the DiBiasi's driveway, wishing that he was someplace else. He took a deep breath as he climbed heavily up the few steps to the front porch.

CHAPTER TWENTY

Emil greeted his lawyer Jacoby at the door very soberly. "Come in Jake; Mama and I were just talking about you. We were thinking of calling you to find out if you knew anything more than we do about that terrible discovery up near our cabin. We just can't believe it." They shook hands as Emil led them into the small sitting room off of the hallway.

Rosemary was sitting there and nodded to Jake as he entered, "Good to see you Mr. Jacoby," she said. "Isn't that an awful thing about those poor girls?"

Jake cleared his throat, twice, then said, "Yes, of course it is. I came here just for the purpose of talking to you both about that. I can't believe what they found."

Rosemary nodded again, her eyes red, as evidence of having just cried; she was very pale and her forehead was wrinkled in a deep frown. Emil took a seat next to Rosemary, and invited Jacoby to take a chair. The couple was eager to hear what Jake might have to say, but Rosemary was the first to question him. "Tell us," she said in a subdued voice, "what's going on, Jake; are we going to be involved in any way with that tragedy?"

"I wish that I could tell you that you won't be involved, I can't, but I don't think that you should worry about it. There are a dozen other cabins in the immediate area besides yours. It's just a coincidence that yours is one of those that is close by. Furthermore, from what I gather from the papers, the speculation is that the girls were murdered elsewhere and taken to the Coconino forest and buried there. That is still only a preliminary hypothesis, a guess. Some have not given up on the idea that two or more homeless men came across the girls while they were hiking or playing in the forest, raped and then killed them to shut them up. That seems to me to be a more logical sequence of events. Jake had a mental flashback, recalling himself standing by as Santos and Ziggy buried the girls. He knew that he should have ordered them to bury the girls in a deeper hole; "Another foot and they would have never been found," Jacoby said to himself.

"But will we be investigated or questioned?" Emil asked. As you know, Rosemary's health is not such that she is prepared to cope with a lot of stress; for that matter, it wouldn't be all that great for me, either. We've never even had to serve any jury duty; we wouldn't be comfortable in a courtroom."

Jake hesitated to reply, knowing that that was a real possibility, but he didn't want to alarm the old folks unnecessarily. "Once they learn who you are, your ages, your life style, and that you are upstanding citizens, any further investigation is unlikely. I can't rule it out, but let's face it, one minute with you two should be sufficient to make them realize that they shouldn't waste their time here. Remember, there are a number of other cabins in the area; I'm sure that the police are checking out the owners of all of the other units. It's routine."

"This is a crazy thought, I know Jake, but Rosemary has wondered if it could be possible that there is any connection between Frankie's murder and those two girls," Emil inquired. "Seems strange that the two crimes that were committed involve our family, one way or another."

Jacoby squirmed a bit uneasily in his chair, and said, "According to the papers, the police have no leads on Frankie's murder, and at this point I believe that they are only speculating about the two girls. There is no reason to believe that the two crimes are connected. I wouldn't be surprised if the authorities found that some homeless men were living in the woods, stumbled across the girls, who might have been hiking, raped them and them killed them to hide their crime. At least that is a logical thing to have happened, in my mind." Emil nodded in agreement, accepting Jacoby's explanation, but he gave no sign that he was really not totally satisfied. He had been a successful construction supervisor, in part because he could anticipate problems and tried to take the proper action before they developed serious consequences; he felt uneasy about Jacoby's explanations. "Maybe there is no connection, Jake, but Rosemary and I have been wondering why someone would kill Frankie, and then these murders pop up. Do you know of anything that Frankie was involved with that would have caused him to be murdered?"

Jake squirmed a little more and slight beads of perspiration peppered his forehead. "I really didn't know Frankie all that well, mostly from meetings with you when he was here. He did do some leg work for me now and then, but not all that much. More recently I had to cut back on that too, because I was gearing down to retire. Not to mention that he was drinking too much and became a little obnoxious at times. I think that he got behind with some bad characters over gambling debts and they got fed up with his stalling on the pay back. That and he probably ticked them off with his big mouth after drinking too much."

Rosemary, almost in a whisper, said, "I never was very happy about him marrying Lucy; always felt uneasy about him. Never really knew what he did for a living, but I'd bet that most of his income came from something shady. Not surprised he got shot."

"Well let's not look for problems," Jake suggested, "the police are working on both cases. Leave it to them. I've got to be going," he said as he rose to leave.

Emil walked him to the front door. "Thanks for coming by, Jake, and let us know if there is any news, about either case."

Jake said, "Will do," as he shook Emil's hand, and left.

The old couple looked at each other, doubt reflected in their faces, and then Emil said, "Well I don't know Mama, I have to wonder."

"I do too," Rosemary softly added.

CHAPTER TWENTY ONE

Detective Orsen Carter was on his hands and knees on a small tarp at the crime scene. The remains of the two bodies had been removed hours before. Carter had a small "digger" in his hand, was leaning into the crevice and probing for anything that might be helpful in solving the murder of the two young girls. As he did so, his right boot gouged out a hole in the muddy soil behind him.

Finding nothing helpful with his digger, he rose and turned to see that his boot had dug a six-inch deep hole in the heavy mud. Carter's eye caught the dull glint of metal; he probed with his digger and uncovered a small, possibly antique pocketknife, the kind that a man might have on his key ring. He pulled it from the mud and knocked off the mud. Wes Mitzer, Carter's partner, saw what Carter had retrieved and asked, "What have you got there Orsen, the weapon?"

"No such luck, Wes, just a small pocket knife, hardly a weapon. It has some engraved design on it; could have come off a key chain; it has a loop on the end. A kid could have dropped it there a long time ago. We'll give it to the lab. Have you found anything worthwhile in your vicinity?"

"Came up empty, so far," Wes responded, "it's so blasted muddy in the whole area, I don't know how we can expect to find anything. I can't believe that you even found that knife. I think that we ought to give it up for today and come back when it dries up a bit. In the meantime, we can put our tape back up to keep out the nosy parkers."

Carter had cleaned up the knife quite a bit and examined it, turning it over several times, and finally said, "I don't think that this knife is going to help us at all; maybe what was left of the clothing might lead us somewhere. Let's pack it up. I'm getting a chill from digging in that icy mud."

Wes didn't argue with that suggestion and began to quietly gather up their tools and other supplies. "I'm cold too partner, he said, "Let's stop by the Lone Pine Restaurant and have some hot coffee, maybe a piece of pie."

"Sounds great," Carter agreed.

The restaurant was only about a mile away, so in just a few minutes they found themselves in a corner booth holding a cup of hot coffee in their two hands. "Ah," Wes sighed, "this is more like it." The waitress added to their pleasure by bringing them the two warmed pieces of apple pie they had ordered. She had convinced them, quite easily, that the pie would taste much better if warmed.

Millie moved with ease, as though she had been serving customers all of her life, which was almost true. She started working at the Lone Pine when she was sixteen, which was eighteen years ago. She was popular with the customers, who were mostly men, because she enjoyed talking to them, and they enjoyed her. Not a beauty, just a wholesome country type gal. As soon as the two detectives entered she had a suspicion as to who they were, and decided to see if they were friendly enough to tell her if there was any news about the "forest murders," which is how the community had begun referring to the crime.

Millie returned to the table to freshen the coffee for the men, and as she filled the cups, she tentatively ventured a question. "Am

I guessing right that you guys are up here looking for clues about the murder of those two girls?"

The two men looked at each other, seemingly not expecting that question. At first there was some hesitation by both of them, but Detective Carter, the senior of the two, finally decided that there was a possibility that there could be some meaningful information to be gained by engaging Millie in conversation. Having read her nametag, he replied to her: "You're pretty observant, Millie, maybe you should be a detective?" She laughed, "Well if you have an opening, I'm ready."

Wes Mitzer responded with a broad grin and asked Millie, "Have you worked here a long time, and do you know most of the folks hereabouts?"

"Sure have, sure do," she answered, "I can call most of them by name, the locals, that is." Then she quickly added, "Of course in the summer we get a ton of folks up here from the valley and elsewhere, even from Sedona. Know a lot of the regulars who come up for the whole summer. Most of them have cabins or double-wides, but we get weekenders and family guests too." The restaurant was fairly quiet at this time of the year and Millie was enjoying standing there talking, with the coffee pot in her right hand while her left hand rested comfortably on her slightly extended hip.

Detective Carter sensed that she was obviously at ease and in no hurry to be occupied with anything else. "So," he interjected, "It doesn't sound like you would suspect any of your customers to be guilty of murder."

Millie took a big breath, and said, "My God, we haven't had anything near that kind of crime since my folks moved up here twenty-two years ago. We have had some theft and a bit of vandalism from time to time; the worst was a major burglary at the post office and then the country club, and that was some time ago. Never had any face to face robberies or physical violence; not here."

Carter was about to ask a question when Millie pointed to a couple who were just entering the eatery. "Gotta go," she said, stepping lively away.

"Whatta ya think, Orsen?" Mitzer asked his partner. "Should we stay awhile and see if we can jog her memory about something that's not in the front of her brain, or should we call it a day and check into that motel in Flagstaff that Marsha reserved for us?"

Carter considered the question for a moment, but he really had already decided to have more coffee and see if Millie could come up with anything at all that might be helpful. "No rush to get there, Wes," he answered, "She might be leaving soon, we don't know, or she might not be in tomorrow; let's probe her a bit more when she comes back...which I'm sure she will; not much business on a Tuesday afternoon. Not to worry, here she comes."

Her brow was slightly wrinkled as she approached the two detectives. "I've been thinking," she said, "Ya know about six months ago, there were three men that came in here together; I had never seen them before and they just didn't seem to fit in with our type of customers. They were different."

Carter's eyes brightened up; perhaps, he thought, their time here would not be wasted. He pursued the opportunity to learn more; "I don't suppose that you could recall what they looked like; you know hair color, weight, height, clothes...anything?"

"I do remember a bit about them. They sat down quickly, all ordered the lunch special posted on the door, never even looked at the menu; I didn't notice when they left; they left cash on the table to pay the bill and the tip. One of them was big, well over two hundred pounds, and one was dressed like a businessman. The third man was more slightly built. Whatever they said to each other couldn't be heard; they were in a corner booth. Oh, another thing; the business man had an unlit cigar in his mouth. I remember that because I told him that he couldn't light up because there was no smoking at inside tables."

Wes asked Millie is she could recall anything about how the other two men were dressed, but she shrugged and said, "Just casual, best I remember, maybe work clothes, but they weren't dirty. Oh, yeah, one other thing I just remembered, I heard one of them call the businessman Mr. Hay or Kay, or something like that."

Detective Carter rose, a signal to Mitzer that they should leave. He dropped a ten-spot on the table, enough to cover the tip, and at the same time said, "Millie, what you have told us may or may not lead us anywhere, but we appreciate your effort in trying to help solve this terrible crime. Please keep this conversation confidential; otherwise it could cause us more problems rather than being of help." Then he advised her, saying, "You can reach either of us through our Phoenix office at this number if something else pops into your mind about those men, or about anyone else that might be a party of interest, as we say. We'll be at the Motel Six tonight and may or may not be back tomorrow. Good coffee."

Millie smiled as she picked up the cash, "Thanks guys; I hope you'll be back." then she waved to them as they left.

CHAPTER TWENTY TWO

Lucy came out of the anesthesia dreaming that she had given birth to a dark haired little boy, but it was no dream. "Are you okay to nurse your baby?" the attendant asked, looking for a positive response.

At that moment Lucy came wide awake, recalling how she had already held her son soon after he was born, and realized that now she was not dreaming. She blinked her eyes once or twice and assured the nurse that she was fully alert. "Yes, yes, I'm fine." The nurse observed Lucy for a moment to confirm that she was awake and alert to what she was doing, then gently laid the baby in Lucy's waiting arms. The new mother easily guided her baby's mouth to her nipple and began to enjoy her new motherhood, grateful that she had had a trouble free, normal delivery. The mental and physical exhaustion she had felt as a consequence of the anticipated delivery and the trauma generated by the death of Frankie had disappeared with the anesthesia. Her life had been turned upside down. Now she felt relaxed, forgetting all of that, and just smiled as she looked down at the little body that had become the dearest thing in her life.

Big brother Al came quietly into the room, carrying a beautiful planter of flowers in full bloom. "Well Sis, looks like you've given me a nephew to take to the ball game in a few years," he said as he leaned over and kissed her gently on the cheek. "A pretty good looking youngster, too."

Lucy looked up at him in admiration, "Oh Al, I am so lucky to have you as a brother. You are always there when one of us is in need. So glad you're here."

"That's what families are all about, Sis," Al replied. He looked at her as though evaluating her mental state, worried that he might cause her further stress if he mentioned the latest disturbing news from Pinewood. She was sure to hear about it from newscasts, he realized, so he decided to talk about it. She was calm; Al's visit had cheered her up and brought color to her cheeks. "You look wonderful, Lucy. The family is relieved that your delivery was easy. Both Mama and Jean had called; Mama talked to one of the nurses and Jean somehow was able to talk to your doctor. They split up the list of calls to everyone, so now the whole family knows that you and the baby are okay; they even know the sex, weight, and length, and are waiting to hear the name you are going to give him. They all agreed not to swarm in here, but they asked me to congratulate you for them, and of course they sent their love by all of these cards they asked me to bring." He laid them next to the planter on the bed table. "You can read them all later."

Lucy continued to nurse her new baby, but was interested is what was going on with the family. "Sit down, Al," she suggested. "Tell me what's new; how are Mama and Papa?"

Al sat, but hesitated for a moment. "The folks are just fine, Sis, but I have some other news that is not too good. I'm not sure about whether I should tell you this or not, but you will likely hear it on the news anyway."

"Don't tell me that they found Frankie's killer, or why it was done. I mean, do tell me if that is the news, or is it something else?" Her eyes were wide open in anticipation of getting answers to the questions that had been burning in her mind.

"Not so far, kiddo, but Frankie's murder is now off of the front page, so to speak, replaced by the discovery of the bodies of two young girls by some Pinewood Sanitary District workmen who were repairing sewer pipes not far from the family cabin. They had moved to a comfortable spot in the forest for their lunch break. Actually, a squirrel uncovered the first small bone while chasing after a tidbit that one of the men had thrown down from his sandwich. A fantastic coincidence. The news did not sit well with Mama and Papa; it's got them all in a snit, but not as badly as the folks all the way from Munds Park to Flagstaff."

"My God! No wonder they're in shock," Lucy exclaimed. "They have been isolated there forever, away from all crime as long as I can remember. That's terrible! Now they will all start locking their places every time they leave; they never had to do that before. What a shame! Are there any suspects at all?" She didn't give Al a chance to answer her question, instead…with a more worried look on her face, she said, "Al, I have been trying to think about why Frankie was killed, and I must admit, I have a concern. I'm not frightened, but do you think that I could be in danger, for some reason? I know enough about crime to know that the way he was shot could mean that it was a mob hit man that did it. I never knew how Frankie made money, really; I just hope that whoever did it doesn't think that I have anything they want, or any so-called secret information. What do you think, Al?"

"I think that you have to put all of those negative thoughts out of your mind, Lucy, and concentrate on being a mother. There are no known suspects in either case as of this moment, and I don't believe that you are in any danger. If the police thought that you were, they would have posted a guard outside of your door here. I'll get Jerry to check out your house every day to see that everything is okay there. Jean said that when you come home, she would spend a lot of time with you, so relax and enjoy your motherhood." He noticed that she had automatically shifted her baby to her other breast, a sign that she had settled down and was doing what he suggested. The news did not totally upset her.

"The detectives are working on both cases now," he added, "so we might hear something soon. I've gotta go, Sis, but I'm so glad for you that everything has gone so well." He leaned over and kissed his sister and the baby gently on their cheeks. He waved as he left the room, saying, "See ya later, keep that milk flowing."

CHAPTER TWENTY THREE

Jim Colby drove up to Munds Park from Phoenix very early in the morning the day after Detectives Carter and Mitzer had ended their first stint at digging in the cold wet mud. He had skipped breakfast in order to avoid the morning commuter traffic, but met Detectives Carter and Mitzer for breakfast in their motel's coffee shop. Not much had been said while they ate, but wiping his mouth with a paper napkin after finishing, Colby said, "Well guys, I hope that my early morning drive up here from the valley will not be wasted. I know you have only been here a short while, but this case has been generating all kinds of media attention. I came up here to get some first hand information, but also to get a feel for what you are doing, and maybe give you some ideas in proceeding with the case. I'm hoping to give the reporters a tidbit or two to keep them off of our backs for a day or two. Can you help me out?"

The two detectives hesitated for a moment, then the senior man, Carter, broke the silence. "Actually, Jim, we expected to have a little more time to do the preliminary work before being quizzed on our findings, but we realize that you are bound to be getting some pressure. The media pounces on crimes like this one like a cat on a mouse. It's really messy out there, but we do plan to examine the area more this morning. I think that we can safely say, however, that the area is not the crime scene; we're confident that the girls were killed elsewhere and then brought to the woods to be buried."

Colby nodded, "I think that that's a correct assumption, however, I have to think that they were murdered in the vicinity, not far from where they were found. They were surely not transported from any distant point. The most logical place to have killed the girls would be in one of the cabins in the close vicinity. I can't see them being shot in a car or truck, and if they were killed at some distant point they would have been buried near that distant point. I know that this sounds gruesome, but it would be logical if the girls were killed in one of the nearby cabins they could have been brought to the site in a wheelbarrow; they were so small and thin it would have been an easy way to transport them. When we investigate some of the cabins we might also be looking at which ones have a wheelbarrow, and then examine them for evidence of use." The two detectives looked at their boss in kind of amazement, but recognized the logic of his scenario.

Carter and Mitzer described their investigation thus far, particularly the interview with Millie, the waitress at the local restaurant, and then turned over the little knife to Colby, which they had put into a small plastic bag. He looked at it briefly, and indicated that he did not see it as a worthwhile clue, certainly not as a weapon. He said that he would turn it over to the Lab boys, just in case that there might be some connection to the crime. "There is always the slim chance that they could find out who owned the little knife, in which case it would prove that they were at the place where the girls were buried. What really does interest me," he volunteered, "is your waitress contact. After you finish your probing of the forest area today, I want you to go back to that restaurant. What's its name?"

"The Lone Pine Restaurant., Wes replied. "I think that it has been operating there for more than twenty years."

"Good," Colby acknowledged, "so there may be more to learn from your Millie, or someone else there. Which reminds me, in talking about this case in the office yesterday, one of my clerks overheard my mentioning the Munds Park murders and came over to ask me about it. It turned out that her folks have a condo in Pinewood and also belong to the Pinewood Country Club. Apparently that is on the other end of the Pinewood community from where you have been digging. She told me that the local semi-volunteer fire department is right next to the country club. It all made me think that we have to open up ourselves to this small, almost isolated community on this case. I want you to go to these facilities as a team, introduce yourselves and let them know that we need their help. I'm sure that they would all like us to solve the crimes as soon as possible, so they can sleep better. My feeling is that we will not get much more to help us from the burial site; we have to look elsewhere, like from your waitress gal at the café. Have a drink and a long dinner there tonight. The more of you they see there, the better chance of learning something that will help us solve these murders. Some other customer may have learned about who you are, and may have a clue of some kind, but be alert to anyone who is just nosy."

"That will mean another night at the motel, plus meals. Is that in our budget?" Carter asked.

"You have the okay; actually for two more nights. By that time, I'm told, that if we don't come up with something, the FBI will be brought in; apparently on the assumption that the girls might have been brought in from out of state for one purpose or another."

"Wes and I are optimistic, boss, that we will get a lead soon," Carter stated, "maybe tomorrow."

"One more thing," Colby suggested, "since probability is that one of the cabins in the near vicinity may have been where the murders were committed. See if you can learn anything about the owners or renters of the cabins within one or two hundred yards from where the girls were found. In the meantime, I'll get Marsha to get on the computer and probe the county records; it could give us the owners' names, but of course, not the renters. You might also stop by one of the realtors' offices and discuss that possibility with them before you get back in the woods. It will give you a bit more time to have the area dry up."

CHAPTER TWENTY FOUR

After visiting Lucy in the hospital, Al felt that he should call his parents and his siblings. He called Connie first and reported on the birth of their new nephew and on how Lucy was doing. "Did she have a normal delivery?" Connie asked, followed by all of the questions a woman would be expected to ask. She was happy to hear that the event was without incident, a normal delivery, and that Lucy was feeling well after giving birth and was breast-feeding her baby. Al informed Connie of the visiting hours, suggesting only that she check with the rest of the family, to avoid having too many visitors at one time. Then Al said that it might be nice if she were to call Jean; thinking that it would be nice if they could visit Lucy together. He also told her that he would be calling both of his brothers, so she would not have to bother, which he soon did.

They had all learned of the killings near the family cabin, but only Gus questioned Al on the event. He was still nervous about any possibility that he may have to talk to the police. "Have they made any progress on the murders of those two girls?" he inquired. "And what about Lucy, have they bothered her at all, or are they going to interview her in the hospital?"

"Not much progress so far as I know," Al responded, "I was able to get in touch with the person in charge of the investigation, Chief Detective Jim Colby. He was pleasant enough, but I sensed that he was not happy at taking another phone call about the double murders. He became more receptive when I explained that my parents owned one of the cabins in the vicinity of where the bodies were discovered. I told him how old our parents are and that they are very disturbed about the crime, and that I was calling to get some kind of assurance that they would not be involved. He understood that I was trying to save them any worry or anxiety over the situation. He informed me that they are investigating the owners and renters of cabins in the area, particularly those in close proximity of where the bodies were found, but he could not promise that Mama and Papa would be spared any questioning. I gave him my phone number and he promised to call me if they did have to talk to the folks. No one from the police has questioned Lucy."

Gus seemed satisfied, but pursued the point by asking another question, which reflected his own anxiety. "Do you think that they will question all of the family members if our cabin was somehow involved in those murders?"

Al, unaware of Gus's illegal drug sales, surprised at the interest Gus was showing in the case, replied to his second inquiry. "The crime scene, or rather the area where the bodies were found, is in the area of the family cabin, that's true, that doesn't necessarily mean that it is close enough to warrant being one of the cabins that the investigators would be checking. I'm sure Papa will hear from them if it is. I really can't see that there is any problem for any of us, other than any inconveniences that we might have if we have to go up there right now, and maybe spend some time with the detectives. The most that I can see happening is that they will check out the cabin ownership, probably contact Papa for confirmation, and then question him as to whether the cabin has been rented out or used by somebody outside of the family. I'm sure that they already know the names of all of our family members, likely have checked them out as well. I know that you and Elaine had talked about going up there with your kids early this year for a short vacation, and I don't see any reason why you should cancel those plans. It's just a routine investigation; if they spend any time in the cabin looking for any kind of evidence, and I can't begin to guess what that might be, I would expect them to be long gone before you and Elaine get up there."

Gus seemed relieved, and said, "That's a good thought, Al. Elaine and I thought that we might have to cancel our plans, but from what you have said, I guess we'll put that worry aside. I think that she will see Lucy as soon as I tell her about the visiting schedule." He said goodbye and nervously hung up the phone; his tic started up again.

"Hell," he thought, "Why should I worry. It's still Mama and Papa's cabin," he reasoned, "no need to have any of us involved." He calmed down a bit, but he knew that he could not take any chances. He would have to exit from his "sideline" and experience the loss of income in the best way he could. They would have to cut back on their life style. He would have to give some thought as to how he could tell his special customers that he could no longer provide their needs. Not a task that he looked forward to, knowing full well that some of them would be very unhappy, and would put pressure on him to continue. He had to think of an excuse that might be acceptable. No matter, it had to be done; the situation with Frankie and now the murders up north were just bringing the police too damn close!

CHAPTER TWENTY FIVE

Detectives Carter and Mitzer, following Jim Colby's direction, found themselves back at the burial site. It had dried up a bit and the slightly warmer temperatures provided a little more comfortable environment to work in than it had been during their first endeavor; however, it was still an unpleasant place to work in. The partners separated, with each one examining half of the area within roughly a hundred feet of the site. Beyond that distance there was heavy forest to the west with cabins starting to the east. The yellow tape that had been staked up around the burial site, probably about two hundred square feet, was still intact, but footprints in the soft ground around that indicated that somebody had been nosing around. The detectives were bothered by that at first, then concluded that the curiosity seekers had all been children; the prints were small and the depressions in the soil were shallow. It did not appear that anyone had crossed the yellow lines. The men searched for more than an hour with no new discoveries, and were both disappointed and discouraged.

Carter was standing, stretching his body to relieve the cramps from being on his knees and stooping. As he looked about him, he became more conscious of the depth of the forest; the trees were close together, leaving no room between them except for the established bike and ATV paths. "Wes," he alerted his partner, "have you thought about the secrets that this forest may hold?"

Mitzer raised his head from a little distance away, pushed himself up from his stooped position and said, "To answer a question with a question, what are you getting at, Orsen?"

"Well looking back into where it is almost dark and the way the trees are clustered, I had a vision of how many Indians may have been buried there years ago, who will never be found. Then my imagination conjured up what other bodies, besides our two young girls, may have been disposed of in there the same way. It could be kind of a secret graveyard."

"Egad, Orsen, do you want to spend more time up here digging for skeletons? All I can think about is getting back down to the warm valley. I've had enough of this."

The verbal exchange was interrupted when Carter's cell phone buzzed. It was Colby. "You and Wes can quit that ground search, Orsen," he directed, "unless you have found something this morning that suggests that you keep looking further. Otherwise I don't think that there is anything more to be gained from that area beyond the little knife that you found. We have the clothes to work on and other avenues I think we can follow."

"That's fine with us, Jim," Carter said, "it's still pretty messy out here. Do you still want us to go back to the Lone Pine Restaurant and see if our waitress gal has recalled any more details about the three men she told us about?"

"Definitely," Colby confirmed, "that was my main reason for calling. See if you can get more of a description of those men, or something on the cars that they must have driven. I have a gut feeling that there has to be a connection between that trio and those poor girls, but we need something solid, my gut feeling won't hack it. Oh, by the way, forensics has affirmed that the girls were shot; they also believe that it was done at close range with a small caliber handgun, probably a 38. No bullet fragments have been found so far, however, so there is no confirmation as to the gun. Shots were to the hearts; passed right through their small bodies.

I'll look for you guys this afternoon. What time do you think you'll be back down to the valley? I want to meet with you both as soon as possible, but I have a meeting right after lunch. Could you make it by three? The meeting should be over by then."

"Carter replied, "Well now that you have given us the okay to quit this mining operation, we can hit the restaurant early and hope that Millie is working today. If we get hung up for one reason or another, I'll call Marsha and give her our ETA, which I would expect to be no later than three thirty...not counting any traffic problems.

"Good," Colby acknowledged, "I hope to have all of the info on the owners and renters in the vicinity of the burial site by the time you check in. It may be a blind alley, but it's an area we have to pursue."

Carter clicked off his phone and turned around to find Mitzer, back on his knees nearby. "Hey partner, what are you doing back in that hole; did you find something interesting?"he asked.

"Sorry pal," Wes responded, "nothing but pine needles and pine cones."

"You can get up now; Colby just called me," Orsen reported, "and said that we can quit the job here. He reconfirmed that he wanted us to see Millie again at the Lone Pine cafe, so we better clean up and get going. Let's hope that she is working today." The men gathered up their stuff together, tramped to their car and headed down to see Millie, looking forward to some more of that good coffee.

CHAPTER TWENTY SIX

When the pair entered the restaurant they were pleased to see that Millie was there; she was pouring coffee for a customer when she spotted them, gave them a short wave and pointed to a vacant table. Both men gave her a nod of understanding and moved to the table she had indicated. Millie walked over quickly, pot still in her hand.

"Welcome back boys," she happily greeted them, "to eat today, or just coffee and more sleuthing?"

"Actually both," Carter replied, "we're hungry, but if you have a few minutes we thought that we might ask you a few more questions...okay?"

Millie looked pleased, obviously enjoying the attention again. "Let me take your orders first, put them in, and then I can sit with you for a bit." The men made their selections from the menus on the table and Millie took them to the "in" spot by the kitchen. Then she came right back to the table, a pot of fresh coffee in one hand and two cups in the other. "I thought that you might like your coffee while we talk," she offered.

"You're a mind reader, Millie," Wes complimented her with a smile. "I think that we're both still a bit chilly from digging around in the woods again; hot coffee will hit the spot." Millie poured the coffee and sat down between them.

"I thought that you would be back, and I've been racking my brain, trying to remember more about those men," she said.

"Anything at all come to mind?" Wes asked.

"Nothing more about the men themselves, but I did remember glancing out the window towards the parking area because the bright orange color of a pickup caught my eye. I didn't give it much thought at the time because a lot of the locals park here if the spaces by the post office are full. It's right across the street, as you've probably noticed."

Carter quickly pursued the point. "Do you think that it belonged to one of those two men?"

"Well all I can say honestly, guys, is that I had never seen an orange colored pickup around here before that time, and I haven't seen one since."

"Anything else, Millie? How about the make?" Wes asked, "Or maybe body damage?"

"I only saw the top half through the window, so I couldn't see too much; if I had to guess, it would be a Ford; that's what most folks around here drive; that or a Dodge. It probably won't help much, but I think that it might have had a triple A sticker on the corner of the windshield."

Carter looked at her quizzically, "Why do you say it might have been?"

"Well, because it was oval, like their insignia, and it had a reddish tint, but it was old and shabby looking, so it could have been any other kind of sticker."

"To be honest, Millie, we may be chasing a rainbow here, those men may have had absolutely nothing to do with the murder of those girls. We have no real evidence at this point, but we will continue our investigation until we can prove one way or another about their involvement, if any. But in the meantime, we would like you to keep our discussions to yourself. We don't want anyone to conclude that we have one or more specific suspects in mind. I probably don't have to say this, Millie, but I guess that I just want to make sure that you recognize the need for discretion in talking about this case. One last quickie question, if you don't mind. If you saw those three men again, would you be able to say that they were the same men who we have been talking about?"

Millie nodded, "I'm sure I could; I've had a lot of practice in getting to know peoples' faces." She then glanced toward the order board and said, "Your lunch is ready, I'll be right back." She returned promptly with the two plates in hand, but she had to leave to take care of other customers coming in for an early dinner or a late lunch.

"A bit iffy, as far as clues go," Wes stated, "unfortunately she had no view of the license plate, so we don't even know in what state it might have been registered."

"The triple A thing is a long shot, but let's see if the office staff can do something with it," Carter suggested. "With so much high-tech and data on computers, they can find out who you were dating in high school. Let's eat up and zip back to headquarters." They ate hurriedly, didn't wait for a bill, and dropped enough cash to cover the charge and a good tip.

On the drive back to Phoenix, they discussed everything that they had learned so far, and they both felt that nothing had really clicked. "Maybe I have been too optimistic about the cabin people; I can't help but think that an owner or renter of one of the cabins in the area has to be involved," Carter mused. "As one of us said early in this investigation, the murders had to have taken place nearby. It isn't reasonable to think that whoever did it hauled the bodies from any distant point. To me it would seem logical that the girls were murdered in one of the cabins close to the edge of the forest."

Jim Colby greeted Carter and Mitzer as they entered the office. "Looks like you two survived the north country all right; any new leads?"

Carter reported that nothing new had been found during their second ground search of the area where the bodies had been found; then he reviewed the brief interrogation of Millie, specifically the orange colored pickup and the windshield sticker in question.

"Wes," Colby directed, "go to the computer section and give them the info on the sticker. It might lead us somewhere. Orsen, I want you to check with the evidence group on that knife; that is still the only real material evidence we have, so far, other than the clothing remnants. The forensics people have determined that the girls were most likely from Mexico, but because they were so young, and had no dental work done, they can't be traced from that direction. We did, as a long shot, send all of the info we had on the bodies to the authorities there. Not much to hope for; young girls disappear down there all the time, and we also realize that there is still the possibility that they could have been from any of the Central American countries."

"But, what about the cabin owners and renters, Jim? Don't we have any data on them yet?" Orsen inquired.

Colby looked disturbed. "Oh hell, I thought that you would have stopped by your desks first, before you came here. There is a report on your desks with the detail on each owner or renter of the eight cabins within 200 yards of the burial site. After you both finish reviewing the report, which I think you should do together, I want to hear your analysis. I'm hoping that you will find some kind of connection to the case. Make some phone calls; maybe visit some of those named at their winter addresses...unless they are out of town, of course. We've got to start making some headway on this case. The top brass is on my ass, and that ain't funny."

"We expected that, Jim," Carter said, "and we'll get right at the reports. With luck we'll have something for you by tomorrow." The detectives left and headed to their respective desks, picking up the reports without hesitating to check for messages as they left. They agreed to meet early the next day in the conference room to review their analysis of the reports.

CHAPTER TWENTY SEVEN

As they spread the report pages on the conference table, Carter said, "Did you notice that none of the seven cabin owners covered in the report live up there year 'round?"

"Yes," Wes answered, "and the one renter has two years left on a five-year lease. The lot numbers have been listed along with the addresses, but I suspect that they all have P. O. Boxes. There is no home delivery up there, other than for UPS or other delivery services."

"I had the thought that it might be worthwhile to talk to the post office people," Carter suggested. "They probably know most of the regulars by sight, name, and box numbers. Just a thought, but right now we've got to work on this report so we can have something to give Jim this afternoon."

The cabins were listed simply in assigned alphabetical order and cross-referenced to the supporting data accordingly, which permitted the detectives to easily discuss details without referring to names and addresses. Cabin "A" was the closest to the crime site, with "B" and "C" on either side. It was noted that the cabins were all well spaced apart from each other, allowing considerable privacy.

"A" is reported as owned by an ATV company and has been used as a business write-off by having customers use the cabin on weekends during the times they ride the rented ATVs through the forest trails. The company principal, J. R. McNaughton, is clean of any criminal offenses according to what the staff could find. No police record, no unsavory connections, no personal or financial problems.

"B" and "C" cabins are owned by a Trust under an Agreement established by Martin and Erin Kelso. "B" is occupied all summer by the Kelso's, but because it is quite small they had "C" built years ago so they could have their three children and six grandchildren spend much of the summer weekends with them. The report states that the utility companies had confirmed that both cabins had seen some winter occupancy in the past, and it was assumed that it was primarily related to skiing at Flagstaff's Snow Bowl.

Cabin "D" is titled in the joint tenancy names of Emil and Rosemary DiBiasi, a retired couple with five adult children, all of whom live in Arizona. Three males, two of which are married, and two married females. The males are Albert, Gus, and Jeremy. The females are Connie (Horton) and Lucy (Salvo). The only member of the group with any police record is Frank J. Salvo, who served a year as a late teenager car thief. He has been clean after that as far as Arizona records are concerned. His only employment in recent years has been as a "leg-man" for a local attorney, a Jake Jacoby. No attempt has been made to investigate Jacoby, other than to confirm that he is a member of the Arizona Bar.

"E" cabin is owned by a widow lady, Shirley Dawson, who lives alone in Ash Fork, Arizona. She has leased her cabin to a single man, Arthur Beck, for five years, which has two years left on the lease. Beck is a salesman for a Flagstaff lumber company. He is a party type, skier, and spends some summer weekends at the cabin. He's had some traffic violations, including a DUI four years ago.

Cabins "F" and "G" are for sale and have been vacant for two years, as per one of the local realtors. The utility companies confirmed the non-usage. Both owners are out of state, one in California, the other in Michigan. Authorities in both states were contacted about the homicides, and reported back that they have informed the cabin owners.

"H" cabin is owned by Charles and Norma Schwartz of Scottsdale, Arizona. They are employed and generally spend only summer weekends at the cabin. They have two children, a 19 year-old girl attending Trinity College in San Antonio, Texas, and a son, 23, serving in the Army, on tour in Iraq.

"Well?" Carter asked his partner, "What do you think? See any prospects for a possible connection with the girls?"

"Nothing really stands out...all very mundane, except for one thing," Wes replied. "I don't know why, but the married name of that DiBiasi daughter, Lucy, makes me think that I should know it."

"You mean Salvo? That is a very common Italian name." All of a sudden, Carter's eyes flashed with recognition. "Wait a minute, partner; I think that we have both been so involved with our own case that we haven't given a thought to what else is going on. Isn't that the same name as the guy that was recently killed in the alley behind a bar in Chandler?"

"Holy crap!" Wes let out; eyes wide. "How could we have missed that connection? Maybe it's just a coincidence, but man, we've got to talk to Jim about it.

Colby will flip over this. It took this report to help us make the tie-in; who would have thought about a Chandler murder and a double homicide in Munds Park?"

"We can't get too excited over this, not yet. It may just be a weird coincidence. We are a long way from determining that the crimes are related, and from knowing how the DiBiasi cabin is involved, if it is," Carter cautioned.

Three o'clock that afternoon found them in Colby's office. He was on the phone and obviously agitated. "We're doing all we can, sir, that's all I can say right now. I may call you back in a few minutes; Carter and Mitzer just came in, maybe they have something." He nodded into the receiver and hung up. "I hope you guys have something we can work on; I'm getting tired of the flack from upstairs."

"We think that we have an interesting revelation that could turn out to be the best lead we have had so far; at least it is an avenue to follow that we did not have before," Orsen replied. "Does the name Frankie Salvo mean anything to you?"

Colby looked confused, but answered, "You mean the guy that was shot dead behind a bar in Chandler recently? What would he have to do with the murder of those two girls?"

The detectives explained to their boss about their findings from the report of owners and renters and the relationship of Frank Salvo to the DiBiasi family, the one that owns one of the cabins near where the bodies were found. Colby's face brightened up; he immediately began to think about how his men could pursue the new lead. "Did you say that Salvo had been a runner or assistant of some kind for a lawyer named Jacoby?"

"That's what the report said," Wes Mitzer answered.

"He, Jacoby, has to be the connection. Get him on the phone right now; if you can't get him at his office, find out where he lives, call him there. If you can't make phone contact today, go to his office and his home. Bring him in for questioning. I want no delay on this guys. He may be one hundred percent innocent of any wrong doing, but we can't take any chances...we have to hit while the iron is hot. Call me as soon as you make contact. In the meantime I'm going to get a warrant issued to search the DiBiasi cabin. With some luck we may recover one or two bullets that could be buried in a wall, piece of furniture, or even the floor. If the girls were shot there I'd bet my badge that the bullets are in that cabin somewhere." The two detectives left in a hurry.

CHAPTER TWENTY EIGHT

Santos got the cash from Jacoby the next morning after their meeting and departed without any further conversation; both were depressed. Back at his one-bedroom apartment in south Phoenix, he looked around to see what he wanted to take with him. Being single, with no family in the area, he was unencumbered by framed photos of anyone or any memorabilia. With no rental lease, he had no financial obligations; the monthly rent was paid through April. He emptied the one dresser in the bedroom of his clean clothes and packed them in his bag-on-wheels, then added his toiletries from the bathroom. He glanced at the dirty clothes in the lid-less hamper, considered the cost of replacing them, but then said out loud, "To hell with 'em." He had no attachment to the apartment, or anything in it; which really described his life.

While he had been driving back from the meeting with Jacoby, he realized that his well-worn old Mercury might not make it to San Francisco. Before he reached his apartment he had made a decision as to how to cope with the car problem. He left the apartment with his bag and stepped next door, into his neighbor's carport. His concern about possibly being observed disappeared as he noticed that the area was deserted.

Knowing that his executive neighbor was on an extended business trip to Korea, he had decided to hot wire his neighbor's car and take it instead of his own, planning to ditch it when he got to California. He got on the interstate 10 and headed to California, melding into the traffic at the same speed as everyone else. He was in no hurry, stopping in Avondale to gas up, and paying in cash.

The traffic was heavy, especially for a Wednesday morning, but it flowed well until lunchtime. Santos pulled into a truck stop, hoping that the stream of cars and trucks would thin out by the time he finished his lunch. Ordering chicken-fried steak and coffee with hardly a glance at the menu, he buried his head in the newspaper he had picked up from the vending machine outside; he was not anxious to engage the waitress in small talk, although at that time of the day she was too busy working to chit chat with anyone. He was grateful to recognize that she was obviously not interested in her 240 pound customer, and hardly gave him a second glance. Finished, he quietly dropped some bills on the table to cover more than the tab, and left.

As Santos moved back into the still heavy traffic, he found that to keep up with everyone else he had to go considerably faster than he felt was safe, about ten miles an hour over the posted speed limit. He was not very comfortable in his borrowed car, which was a newer car, but a little smaller than he would have liked. The seat didn't retract as fully as his own car, and did not provide enough room for his long legs; he felt cramped. Still, the car had a lot more power than his own.

"To hell with Jacoby," he thought as he continued his drive. "He'll never see me again. I've taken all the risks; let him sweat out whatever happens up north. The Mexican deal is dead anyway." He considered stopping again before he got to San Francisco to call his sister. She had no idea that he planned to visit her, or maybe live with her for a while. He cancelled the thought; no need for another chance that someone might identify him later.

He wanted to remain anonymous. He would get his wish, in a tragic way.

Traveling at 75 to 80 miles an hour, with heavy traffic on each side of his car, a line behind him and a gasoline truck ahead of him, he suddenly got a cramp in his right leg. It was immediately very painful and immobilized his leg. He swore and groaned simultaneously. There was no way he could stop the car or move out of his position. He brought his left knee up to try to steer by it while he reached down to massage his right calf. As he did so, the cramp invaded his thigh, he almost screamed with the pain. He panicked as he had a flashback to when his younger brother drowned in a neighborhood swimming pool because he was struck with severe stomach cramps, and couldn't swim.

Jerkily, his right foot came off of the gas pedal, and then clipped the brake pedal. The car jumped and skidded just enough to cause the trailing auto, which was following too closely, to ram into Santos' car, pushing it violently into the gasoline carrier. All three vehicles exploded into a ball of flame. It was an immediate inferno.

All traffic behind the fire came to a standstill; cars skidded all over and unto the shoulder of the road. Police arrived from somewhere in minutes; fire truck sirens were blasting as they sped to the scene. It was chaotic. Fortunately, the truck driver had only minor injuries, he had escaped the cab quickly after the collision, but the car behind Santos was totaled, and the driver was eventually taken away in an ambulance with burns and expected internal injuries. His airbag had saved his life. Santos, jammed in between the other two vehicles, died upon impact; his airbag never functioned; he was incinerated.

After the flames were extinguished, the firemen and the police had the gruesome task of removing what was left of his body, and then trying to find something that would help to identify the victim. All of Santos' clothing was gone, wallet, money, and papers destroyed. The remains were taken to the morgue, and listed as John Doe.

No one would ever know what happened to Hugo Santos. His sister never learned of his death. Jacoby never heard from him, and assumed that he was probably in prison, and really didn't give a damn. Santos had disappeared from the face of the earth, and no one cared. He was nothing more than a period at the end of a useless life.

CHAPTER TWENTY NINE

Jim Colby buzzed his secretary, "Marsha, see if Carter and Mitzer are in the office. If they are, have them come see me as soon as possible." Marsha found that both detectives were available and in five minutes they found themselves seated in front of Colby's desk.

"We were just getting our notes together, boss, and were practically on our way to your office when Marsha collared us. Guess you're anxious to hear about Jacoby," Carter said as the two men walked toward the conference chairs and sat down.

"I wish we had some positive news, Jim, but we don't; however, from what we have investigated we believe that your conclusion that Jacoby has to be involved is correct. We checked out his office, he was not there and it appeared to us that there is no activity going on there. We also went to his apartment, gained entry through the courtesy of the building manager, and found several days of mail on the floor in front of the door slot. We think he's flown the coop; right Wes?"

"That's what we have concluded," Wes agreed, "and the fact that the manager said that he had not seen Jacoby for about two days seems to confirm our conclusion."

"Do we have the license number of his car, the car make, model, and year?" Jim Colby questioned.

"We have the MVD working on that right now, and we should be getting a report back in the next hour or so," Wes replied.

"Okay; as soon as you receive that info arrange for an all points for Mr. Jacoby. If he is involved, he is probably on his way out of the state, and maybe out of the country. To keep you fellas informed, I should tell you that we are also working on that triple A sticker thing; their offices have been informed about the case, given the data we have on the truck, and they will let us know if they can ID the owner and the vehicle. Slim chance, but who knows."

"Wes asked, "What about the clothes? What about the antique knife? Anything?"

"Not yet," Colby answered, "but we should hear something soon. I had another idea last night; couldn't sleep thinking about those girls. I got thinking about that orange colored truck, wondering if it might have been in some kind of accident and was being re-painted. The orange color could have been just the primer coat; who would ever paint their truck orange? Maybe a teenager's car, but not a truck. I think Millie saw a primer coat; the owner has probably already taken the truck back to the body shop for the final coat. Check out all auto body repair and paint shops on the east side, especially in Mesa and Chandler; that area seems more likely to produce results. The job was most likely finished in the last six months. Save the chasing around, see what you can do over the phone. Split up the list, and keep me posted on anything that sounds interesting. "

The detectives nodded to their boss and headed to their respective desks after agreeing that Mitzer would take the A to L commercial telephone book listings, and Carter would take the M to Z listings. Both men seemed more optimistic than ever about the new lead furnished by Colby. Carter reflected, "Why didn't one of us think about the orange color being a primer. That's almost a no-brainer."

"That's why Colby is the boss," Wes added.

Wes was halfway through his list when he got a call back from a small body shop in Mesa that had repaired a Ford pickup a few months ago and had put only a primer coat on the truck until just a few weeks ago. He walked over to his partner's desk and filled him in, but said, "Why don't we follow this up in person right now, but wait to tell Colby. If it turns out to be a solid lead he will be happy; if not, he won't be disappointed."

"Boy, you're getting to be a psychologist, partner," Orsen responded. "However, I can't disagree with your thinking. Let's go."

At the address was "Art's Body Shop," and the long-time owner, Art Gibson, proved to be very helpful. Although in his mid sixties, his memory was excellent. "I wasn't real happy to do that job," he said. "I had a suspicion that the truck had been in an unreported accident, but I didn't push it with the customer. He didn't look like the type that I would want to argue with; besides he negotiated a cash price with me. He paid for the entire job back when he first brought in the truck. I thought that something had happened to him, but then he came by last month and had me put on the final coat. The primer had weathered a little so we had to freshen it up a bit, but I didn't charge him any more since he had paid up ahead anyway."

Carter and Mitzer smiled at each other, as if to say, "This is it...we're on the man's tail!" "Could you give us a description of the man?" Carter asked. "Tall? Short? Fat? Hair color? Name? Anything?"

"Happy to oblige," Art complied, "If he is a criminal, I would love to see him put away. Anyway, he had a thin build, not very tall, with a Latino appearance; had a small mustache. Didn't give his last name; told me just to call him Ziggy. Crazy name, but it must be a nickname; no mother I know would name their son Ziggy."

"How about age?" Wes inquired.

Art hedged a bit, not being a good judge of ages, but finally said, "My guess would be somewhere between thirty and forty."

"Good enough, Art, but now we need some numbers, which you should have in your records...at least they should be, particularly the license plate numbers and the VIN." Art excused himself for a minute to get the information from his records and returned to the two men with a little smile on his face and a slip of paper containing the numbers requested, which also confirmed that the vehicle was licensed in the state of Arizona. Wes took the slip of paper, but noting the smile on Art's face, he asked, "Was there something else, Art? You seem happy about something."

"I had made a notation in my records, don't really know what I had in mind, but when we worked on that truck I found an old envelope in the glove compartment that had an address on it; it was addressed to just Mr. Ziggy. Maybe I thought that I would have to call him if he didn't come back for the final paint coat. Time went by and I forgot all about it until he finally did come in. I thought that you might find it helpful, so I wrote the address on the back of that paper; it's someplace in Chandler."

The two detectives grinned at each other, and Carter stuck out his hand to Art and said, "Art, you may have given us the best lead we have had in this case. Without this address, which may lead us to one of the killers, we would have a tough time tracking down Mr. Ziggy. If it works out, one of us will let you know if you are a hero." He and Art both laughed, and Wes joined in; all of them realizing that the address on that envelope could be of real value in solving the murder of two young girls. The detectives left on a high note, anxious to meet with their superior, Jim Colby.

CHAPTER THIRTY

Al DiBiasi sat quietly at a corner table at Coco's, waiting for his younger brother Jerry, who had requested that Al meet with him at the restaurant. He gently stirred his cup of coffee with a teaspoon and pondered why Jerry wanted to meet with him alone. He mentally explored the possible reasons and decided that it had to be one of two: Jerry needs money again, or he has gotten some young chick pregnant. Al had loaned his brother some money in the past and concluded that that was the more likely reason for the meeting. Just then Jerry walked to the corner table.

"Hi big brother," he said in a less than casual way, "thanks for meeting me."

Al rose to shake his brother's hand, "No problem kid; I think that the crew at the post office is always glad to see me gone once in awhile. I just had a sandwich; you want some lunch?"

"Coffee would be fine, Al," Jerry answered, "had a burger on the fly a minute ago."

Al waved his waitress over and ordered Jerry his decaf and a warm-over for himself while Jerry settled into the booth facing Al, who realized from his brother's countenance that something serious was in the wind.

"I take it from the frown on your face," Al started, "that you are not a happy camper for some reason or another. Money problems?"

"Not this time dear brother. I need your advice on something, but you have to promise me that what I have to tell you will not be passed on to Lucy or Mama and Papa. It has to be kept out of the family. You will understand when I explain it to you."

Al's dark eyebrows arched as if in question. "Well Jerry, I will promise to keep whatever you tell me in confidence, with the exception being that if I believe it to be detrimental to the family, or any close friends, I would have to reconsider. If so, I would discuss it with you before I relate the circumstances to anyone. You understand?"

"I do Al, and I appreciate your honesty. Let's leave it at that. This is something I feel guilty about, and believe that unless I admit to it, to someone now, it may be revealed later and become a more serious problem. It could also cause some embarrassment to the family and to Lucy."

"My God, Jerry, this sounds really dramatic. Are you sure you want to tell me whatever it is? If it is criminal, maybe you should be talking to the police."

"Maybe I will have to Al, but right now I just feel that I need your guidance. In a nutshell, I know that Frankie was involved with someone who got young girls from Mexico and more or less sold them to so-called dealers in the Phoenix area and other southwest states. The dealers, really pimps, worked them for income. They were kept isolated; most could not even speak English."

Al took a deep breath, giving himself a minute to have what his brother said to sink in, and to withhold his shock. "I didn't think that you and Frankie were all that close, or that he would tell you all about his illicit activities. Which, by the way, I guess should really come as no great surprise; Jean and I often wondered about his income and what he did for a living. He always seemed to have a lot of free time. Maybe I was envious. Did Frankie draw you into the business?"

"No," Jerry shamefacedly acknowledged, "but I was a good customer, and Frankie always made sure that I got what he called the cream of the crop, and he charged me less than the market price. Now you have to realize that I could be in trouble with the police if they discover what Frankie was doing, and that I was involved. He had his own string of girls, which I think was his main source of income."

"Wow Jerry! That is a blockbuster. I had no idea that you and Frankie had any connection outside of family dinners or meetings. Are you asking me if you should go to the police, or just keep quiet? On the hopes, of course, that it will all never be revealed?"

"Yes, Al, that's exactly what I am asking you to do, unless you have some other idea about what I should do. I'm at a loss."

"First of all, Jerry, I intend to keep this between us for the time being. We'll have to wait and see how things work out with the police on solving Frankie's murder, and whether his activity had a connection with the deaths of those two girls. I don't believe that you are obligated to go to the police at this time, but you have to realize that you may be called in if they make some connection with you, even as just a customer. You must have some real apprehension now that the bodies of the girls have been found. This sheds a whole new light on Frankie, although it could still turn out that those murders had nothing to do with Frankie himself. This all boggles my mind; don't do anything for the moment. Give me a little time to consider your exposure, what this could mean to Lucy and the folks. I have to think a bit more about this. The murders, as far as I know from the news reports, seem to be two separate crimes; if so, it may not be too bad for the family. Go home, Jerry: I'll call you tomorrow."

"I'm sorry about bringing you into this, Al; I just didn't know who else I could talk to about it all. Thanks for your time; I'm lucky to have you as a brother." Jerry rose, shook Al's hand and left quietly while Al sat and slowly stirred his cold coffee.

CHAPTER THIRTY ONE

The two detectives, Orsen Carter and Wes Mitzer, sat in the small conference room and reviewed their meeting with Art Gibson. They had to write up a report for Jim Colby and for the file being built on the murder case of the two girls. They were both excited about the results of their meeting at the body shop and their good luck in locating the shop in the first place. They were anxious to see what kind of reaction they would get from Colby when he received the news, but as it turned out, he took the news calmly.

"That was great detective work, men, and it may turn out to be the biggest lead yet, but I've seen too many good leads over the years that just seem to evaporate, so I try not to get too excited too soon. This sounds very encouraging; however, we have a long way to go. This Ziggy thing and the pickup truck may be just leading us down the primrose path, a dead end. Let's keep our cool."

Wes interrupted his boss, "But don't you think that we should get on the address thing right away, Jim? It would seem that the sooner we check out that address and see if he is still there, the sooner we can either move on him or chase after him at some forwarded address."

"Of course, Wes; I was getting to that," Colby replied, "First things first, and I do want you both to head to that address as soon as you leave here. However, you should have a little more information. Marsha should be getting more information on her computer right now from the MVD. From the VIN numbers you got from that body shop guy, they have already identified the vehicle for us as a 2004 Ford Pickup truck, which confirms the description you received from the shop owner. Before you leave we will have Mr. Ziggy's surname confirmed; we will have all the data on his driver's license; weight, height, hair color, etc. Unless," Colby paused, "the address you gave us is incorrect. Also, it could be an old address of his, in which case it will take a lot longer to track him down. Marsha has already worked the reverse name/address telephone directory; she should be about done. Oh, here she is, with some good info, I hope."

"Mr. Colby," Marsha started as she came into the office. Then she looked at Carter and Mitzer and said, "You guys will be happy to hear this too; we made a hit. The directory has a Z. Rios at that Chandler address the boys brought in. That's got to be your Mr. Ziggy," she beamed. "I also got the driver's license data from DMV, and that man sure doesn't look like a tough killer to me." She gave Colby and each detective a copy of the computer printout, which included a copy of Rios' driver's license picture.

"Thanks, Marsha," but you should know by now that killers come with all kinds of faces and personalities, some look like Mormon Tabernacle Choir boys. I don't think that you would consider dating Ziggy, even if he came to pick you up in a tux and in a limo." She laughed as she left the office, giving them all thumbs up.

"Well men, with what we have now, I think we can identify Mr. Ziggy, once he is spotted. While you two are checking his residence, I'm going to have an APB issued for his arrest, based on suspicion of murder. I think that you know that we have been hoping to hear back from the Mexican authorities as to the girls. They are accustomed to having young girls missing down there all the time. We informed them that the clothing remnants indicated that the girls were most likely from south of our border, but it would be nice if we could get some kind of confirmation from them. If we get any information from them that is worth following up on, we may have to send one or both of you down there. I know that their budget problems are at least as bad as ours, if not worse, so they may not oblige us by sending someone up here to help us with this case. To split the difference, cost wise, we may compromise and meet them in Tucson. Of course this thinking all depends on whether they come up with something, or not. If they come up with a zero, there will be no meeting, anywhere…but I'm hopeful. Now, do you two have any questions: No? Well then, nuff said, get going."

CHAPTER THIRTY TWO

At Zoe's Barber Shop on east Chandler Boulevard, Ziggy Rios sat comfortably in Jose's chair, the third and last chair before the back door exit. Jose always cut Ziggy's hair, or did so for the last two or three years, and they had established an easy man-on-the-street relationship. Jose was a sports fan, a non-political person, and always had something to say about the latest sports event, be it an Arizona Cardinals' game, the Sun's last blowout, or even the rumors of the Coyotes possible sale. Today he was unusually quiet, for one reason or another.

"Cut it a bit on the short side, Jose," Ziggy directed; "I've got to go south for awhile; don't know when I'll get back."

"Sure thing, Ziggy," Jose responded. "You want the sideburns short too?"

"Yea, go ahead; I don't want those whackos in Mexico chopping me up." He had made up his mind that this was going to be his last stop before leaving for Hermosillo, his hometown in Sonora, Mexico. The truck was all gassed up and parked behind the barbershop, as usual. He always parked it there so he could enter and leave from the back door.

Jose finally found his tongue and began rambling on about how bad the "reffing" was at last night's Sun's game, but Ziggy wasn't paying any attention. His mind was on getting away from Phoenix before the police learned of his involvement with the two dead girls. He consoled himself, believing that the only way a connection with him could be made would have to be through Santos or Jacoby. "I'd bet Jacoby is in Canada right now," he reasoned, "and Santos should be in San Francisco with his sister." He believed that his only worry should be to avoid a traffic violation as he left Arizona. He reminded himself that the state was using a lot of cameras on some of the main drags.

Ziggy was jolted, almost out of his seat, as his reverie was broken by the sight of a well dressed man crossing the street, headed right for the barber shop. Call it his instincts, or whatever, but he immediately sensed that the man was a plainclothes detective. Ziggy's experiences had developed in him another sense, similar to how a British salesperson can immediately spot an American tourist.

Jose was unaware of what was happening, and said,"Hey, Ziggy, what's wrong? You're moving too much."

"Sorry, Jose, I gotta go. I'll be back." With that he jumped off of the chair, threw the towel at Jose, and was at the back door before Detective Carter entered the front door. Carter had seen Ziggy leave the chair through the big glass window, drew his gun as he entered the shop and was halfway to the back door by the time Ziggy got there himself.

Waiting outside of the back door, as Ziggy pushed it open in a panic, was Detective Mitzer. Ziggy almost fell right into the detective's arms, who said, "Well, what do we have here?" as he put Ziggy into an arm lock.

Orsen Carter was right at Ziggy's back and pressed his gun into the man's spine, hard. Ziggy wilted for a moment, then became defiant and tried to play games. "What the hell is this? A robbery? Here take my wallet." He twisted around in an attempt to reach into his back pocket.

"Stop right there Mr. Rios;" Carter ordered, "You are Ziggy Rios aren't you? No, this is not a robbery," he continued, "I am

Detective Orsen Carter, and my partner is Detective Wes Mitzer." Both men flashed their ID cards in Ziggy's face.

"Yea, yea, that's my name," Ziggy antagonistically replied. "So what?!"

"Murder is what, mister smart ass," Carter confidently answered. "Now we have the privilege of taking you downtown for a little conference, during which, for your own good, you might tell us where your lawyer friend, Mr. Jacoby can be found. We know that you, Jacoby, and one other man were involved with the murder of two young girls in Munds Park. We'll read you your rights on the way downtown. Don't worry about your hair; we'll see that it gets trimmed nicely," he laughed.

By the time they got to the station, Ziggy Rios was like a wet noodle; he sat in the back of the detective's car almost cowering and muttering to himself. He submitted meekly to being finger printed and answered the booking questions without any challenge. Even before he could be transferred to a holding cell, Jim Colby learned of his arrest and ordered him to be brought to his office.

Colby reviewed the case of the two murdered girls and the evidence that they had against Rios, who sat slumped in the conference chair in front of Colby's desk. "We are, at this moment, Mr. Rios," Colby said, "running a check on your background… if you have a record, what time you may have served, what your occupations have been, where you have lived, who you have associated with, everything. We know a lot already, but by the time we finish we will know where you buy your gas. So whatever you tell us now may be of benefit to you when it comes time for indictments. We are particularly interested in your partners; we know that there were three men involved in those murders."

Rios looked perplexed, nervous, and unsure of what he should say, and wishing that Mr. Jacoby was there to tell him what to say, or do. He finally decided to ask for an attorney. "Can I call my lawyer now?" he asked.

At that moment Mr. Jacoby was sitting in his office, trying… unsuccessfully, to get Ziggy over the phone; with no answering machine hook-up on the other end, he could not leave a message. Not having heard from Santos, he had hoped that Ziggy may have heard if Santos had gotten settled down with his sister in California. Jacoby put the phone down after eight rings, giving up the thought of making contact, and made himself believe that Ziggy had probably returned to his family in Mexico. All that he had to do, he thought, was to play it cool; generate some legal work for Sandy, who knew nothing, really, about the Mexican "imports." With bankruptcies on the rise, Jacoby concluded that that area of possible legal work would be the easiest and quickest way to drum up some business. The ringing of his phone startled Jacoby; he picked it up and answered;

"Jake Jacoby." It was Sandy.

"Oh I'm so glad you're in Mr. J." she said excitedly, "I just got a call from Ziggy, who said he couldn't reach you, so he called me. There's some kind of problem and he is under arrest or something like that. He wasn't too clear on whether he needs bail or not, but he is in the county jail, downtown." She was breathless when she finished.

Jacoby sat stunned, his mind racing over the possibilities as to what Ziggy may have done to get himself arrested. Was he speeding? Was he drunk? What did he say to the police, if anything that might have involved him or Santos? He tried to calm himself, but suddenly he was struck with fear. After taking a few breaths, slowly, he said, "I'm glad you called me, Sandy. I suspect Ziggy was speeding and maybe had a couple of drinks. I'll take care of it. I was going to call you anyway. I've got to go to California on some business and will be gone for about ten days. The office can stay closed, so you take off until I get back. I'll give you a ring when I return."

"Oh, thanks Mr. J." Sandy happily replied. "I hope you get Ziggy out of jail. He was pretty upset. Enjoy California." She hung up and Jacoby sat there, the phone dangling from his hand…

visibly shaken. He slowly placed the receiver back in its cradle. He unwrapped a fresh cigar, automatically placed it in his mouth, but made no effort to light it, as though he would not get any pleasure from doing so. His mind was filled with dire thoughts; his enterprise was falling apart and he felt depressed, confused.

CHAPTER THIRTY THREE

At the scene where Santos died a clean-up crew placed parts of the vehicles in a flatbed truck with short sides, to keep the pieces from falling off. Witnesses had confirmed that the driver of the sedan had been at fault, so the police were hoping to find something that would help identify the driver, assuming that some lawyer would be looking for someone, or some company, to bear the legal liability for the horrific accident.

"Hey guys," one young man signaled his fellow workers, "look what I found."

"What is it?" a companion questioned.

"A smudged calling card, just burnt around the edges," the finder answered. "It was just lying on the ground, partially under one of the burned tires."

Another worker said, "Maybe it was there all the time. It may have nothing to do with the drivers of the three vehicles."

"Well I think that we better give it to a policeman, if we can find one," the finder said. "You never know; besides that, maybe there will be a reward or something."

"Don't hold your breath," his fellow worker said sarcastically; "I think we'll have to find something better than that."

"Well you guys keep humping, I'm going over there by the police car. One of those cops looks like the head honcho; maybe he'll think that the card could be useful, one way or another. I'll be right back." He walked over to Sergeant Doyle and handed him the card. "Officer, this is the only thing we have found, so far, that might help to identify one of the drivers. Think it might help?" he asked.

The sergeant took the card and examined it briefly, "Well there's always a chance, thanks. It looks like it must have belonged to a lawyer, the "at law" part is pretty visible, and so is part of the name. It looks like Jacob, or something like it. "What's your name?'

"Harlan Reed, sir," the finder replied.

"Thanks again for finding the card, Harlan. I don't know if it will help us or not. We'll have some lab folks work on the phone and fax numbers to see if they can be used. Someone may contact you later for verification of the find if it becomes useful, but what we would really like to have, if you can find it, is the license plate to the sedan, that sure as hell didn't get burned up."

Harlan returned to the work area with renewed vigor, and informed his fellow workers about what the sergeant had said, and that they should zero in on trying to find the license plate of the sedan.

Sergeant Doyle put the card in a small zip-lock baggie and returned to his car, which he started up and headed right to the police headquarters in Barstow.

At Barstow, the lab department put the damaged calling card into a chemical solution and then under a microscope. Technician Trish Taylor, in less than a minute let out a happy sounding "Wall-la!" which meant to those nearby that she had gotten a good read on the card. "Jake Jacoby, Attorney at Law," Trish announced to no one in particular, but then turned her head towards her supervisor, who was standing close by.

"But only got a P. O. Box number in Phoenix; no street address. However, I did get a complete 602 phone number." That got her supervisor's attention, and he quickly directed her to print out the data on her computer and then relay it directly to Sergeant Doyle, or his office, which she did.

Doyle's assistant read the card data from her computer screen, printed out a copy for the sergeant and put it on his desk. Along with the card information, there was also an explanation as to where, when, and how the card was found. When Doyle got back to his desk and read the message, he directed his assistant to call the phone number given on the card. There was no personal response to the call, but a phone recording confirmed the card information, with a man's voice and the usual "will return your call as soon as possible." With that information, Doyle leaned back in his chair and considered all of the possible reasons why the lawyer's card should have been found where it was. Was the card there all the time, before the accident? Was it in the possession of one of the drivers? If so, why? Had one of them employed Mr. Jacoby for a divorce or other legal work? "I think that I better call the Phoenix police, give them all of the information I have, and let them carry the ball. Maybe they can make the connection," he said to himself.

CHAPTER THIRTY FOUR

Jacoby, unaware of the progress that the police had made in solving the two crimes, was able to pass through the routine checkpoint upon entering the jail without being challenged. The departmental communications had also not been given to the jail personnel that would have prohibited him from meeting with his "client", or caused him to be arrested. He met with Ziggy Rios in a small private meeting room, and Ziggy nervously detailed how he was arrested and explained, rather vaguely, the proposed charges against him. He said that he was told that the charges would have to be filed within twenty-four hours or they would have to let him go. He said they laughed when they told him that, so he presumed that he would not be released.

"That's right, Ziggy, but they may hold you on charges other than anything connected to the girls, which would give them more time to firm up their case, if they really have one. What have you told them?" Jacoby inquired.

"Nothing, Mr. J., I actually told them to go screw themselves. I think they're bluffing about that waitress at the Lone Pine Restaurant having seen my truck up there."

Jacoby looked Ziggy straight in the eye, caught a little evasiveness in his face and felt that something was wrong; he asked, "Did you call Mexico and our three distributors like I asked you to do?"

Ziggy lied, "Of course boss, as soon as you left the office," but Jacoby could feel the lie.

"Okay, Ziggy; I'll check back with you this afternoon, and if bail is needed, I'll post it for you. You could be out of here by tomorrow. Play it cool, stay calm, and let them do the talking; the less said the better."

"Couldn't be soon enough; I hate this place," Ziggy said, reflecting his anxiety.

Jacoby left him there, did not even shake his hand or say goodbye. He knew that Ziggy would sell his soul to save himself, and by tomorrow he would be singing like a canary. Jake recalled the sharpness of the Lone Pine waitress; she would be reliable, and like all good waiters and waitresses, she undoubtedly had a good memory. If she said she saw that truck, she saw it. He recalled how she had told him not to light up his cigar; a moment, he was sure, she also would not have forgotten.

Meanwhile, at Jacoby's office, which he had gained entrance to via the office complex's manager; Colby stood at the doorway, and was surprised at the sparseness of the facility. He did not know that Jacoby had been gradually closing down his legal practice. He went to the one four-drawer file cabinet and found a few file folders in the top drawer, one of which got his attention; it was headed "Emil and Rosemary DiBiasi." He recalled that that was a name from the Frankie Salvo murder case. Reading what was in the folder, he concluded that Jacoby's connection with the DiBiasi's was principally legal work related to the preparation of a Will, with copies of documents drawn up on a method to dispose of the family cabin, post mortem.

Colby called the phone number in the file and arranged to meet the couple at their home in an hour, and received directions to the home from Emil. He gave Emil just a simple explanation for the meeting, which was that he wanted to have further confirmation of their relationship with their attorney, Mr. Jake Jacoby. He actually hoped to learn more about the lawyer, something that might help solve the double murders. The request for a meeting sounded serious to Emil, so he called Al and asked if he could join in the meeting; Al agreed.

Upon being greeted by both Emil and Al, and then being introduced to Rosemary, Colby identified himself and repeated the objective of the meeting, but Emil interjected an invitation. Although Emil knew that this was to be an official meeting, his Italian hospitality character forced him to offer the Chief Detective a glass of Chianti. Colby, sensed the need to put the old couple at ease, he had felt their anxiety, accepted the offer and joined them and Al for a moment in discussing the weather. After a sip or two of the wine, he reintroduced the reason for his visit. In just a few minutes, it was confirmed that they had employed Mr. Jacoby over the last few years to help them with various legal problems, but more recently in relation to preparing their Will. They did add that he had visited them yesterday or the day before, they weren't sure which, and discussed the crime that occurred near their cabin in Munds Park. They said that he was there to give them assurance that they should not expect the police to involve them. They admitted that they were surprised that he had called on them, and they were both unsure of what to think about his statements. The old couple was still a bit nervous, and wondered why Mr. Jacoby would have anything to do with the crime.

Rosemary rather timidly ventured a question, "Why are you inquiring about Mr. Jacoby? He is a lawyer; surely he would not be involved with anything like a murder."

Al had been tormenting himself, mentally, about Jacoby and finally vented his opinion about the man. "Mama, Papa, I believe that Mr. Colby may be on the right track."

Mr. DiBiasi spoke up; "What do you mean, son? Tell us."

Al shifted in his chair, not quite sure about what he should say, but he went on. "As much as I hate to suggest it, because of our close family, I have a gut feeling that there is family involvement in the murders, although not directly."

"What?!" the parents exclaimed simultaneously, in horror.

Al went on to reveal Jerry's activity with Frankie Salvo, and Jerry's suspicions that Frankie had a business connection of sorts with Jacoby. "I have no proof of any wrong doing, and I guess that you might call my comments as hearsay. However, I do think that you, Mr. Colby, might want to talk to Jerry, and also our sister Lucy, Frankie's widow. I'm sure you know about Frankie, and how he was killed."

"Of course," Colby confirmed, "I have worked with the detectives on that case and we just recently made the connection with your family, in terms of how he was related to all of you. For a while we were pursuing the Salvo name. We do know about Lucy, but our investigations have not shown that she had any knowledge about anything criminal that Frankie may have been involved with. She is apparently a nice, but rather naïve housewife. We know Frankie was involved with gambling, and that he did owe some money to unsavory people. Yet, we have not connected his murder to any gambling problems. There is a knowledge gap there somewhere. We feel that there was another purpose in putting him away. Now we believe that only Mr. Jacoby may have the answer to that question."

Al seemed relieved that Colby was putting all the pieces together, whether or not it would be unpleasant for the family. "If you would like me to, Mr. Colby, I could have Jerry meet us at Lucy's home. She just had a baby, but should be home by tomorrow; my wife, Jean, will be with her. I would be glad to call them and set up the meeting." Colby was pleased to have Al make the calls and a date and time were established, subject to Lucy's availability.

Colby thanked the DiBiasi's for their time, and the wine, and promised them that they would not be involved any more than necessary. He said goodbye to the three of them, and said to Al,"I'll look for your call to confirm the meeting; thanks again."

And he left. Al kissed his mother and shook his father's hand, and also departed.

The old couple looked at each other as if to say, "What the hell is happening to our family?" Emil gazed over at Rosemary, who looked a bit dazed. "We can't do much about what's happening, Mama. Let's forget it and have another glass of wine."

Rosemary's eyes brightened up and she agreed, "Why not?" she said, and they did. Both dozed off in their recliners.

CHAPTER THIRTY FIVE

Jim Colby answered his phone on the first ring and was surprised to hear a heavy Latino accented voice, informing Colby that the caller was Lieutenant Rodriquez from the Mexico City police department, who asked if the Phoenix police had any information on a Ziggy Rios. Colby's eyes lit up with excitement; "Yes, Lieutenant, we certainly do; in fact we just recently took him into custody, but have not yet charged him with a crime. I'm hoping that you have some information that will help to settle that question."

The Lieutenant spoke perfect English, and responded that they had arrested two men for running a prostitution ring that used teenage girls, some even younger. He said that they also had evidence that some of the girls had been transported to the United States, more specifically, to Phoenix. The contact in the states, he said was Mr. Ziggy Rios.

Colby nearly jumped out of his seat. "Lieutenant Rodriquez, you cannot believe how happy you have made my day." He went on to explain about the difficulties his department has had in solving the murders of two young girls, both of whom were believed to have come from Mexico. "Up until now, Lieutenant, the solid evidence has been skimpy, and we were to the point that our best hope for a conviction would have to be a confession from Rios."

Rodriquez, always eager to take a trip paid for by his department, suggested that he meet with Colby in Phoenix and bring the tapes covering the interrogations of the two Mexicans that had been arrested, along with other information relative to the prostitution ring. Colby quickly agreed, and the Lieutenant promised that he would be in Colby's office by noon of the next day.

Lieutenant Rodriquez kept his promise, and enjoyed the opportunity to expand on his department's expertise in investigating and arresting those who were guilty of operating the prostitution ring and "sale" of girls to Mr. Rios. Colby, seeing the pride of the Mexican officer in detailing the arrests, sat back and allowed the officer his moment of braggadocio, who also confirmed that they had established that all transactions with Mr. Rios had been in cash.

At that point, Colby called to have Rios brought into his office. Confronted with the evidence furnished by the Mexican officer, Rios paled and nearly collapsed, and said,

"I think I need a lawyer." He had come to the realization that Jacoby would not be around to be of any help. Colby agreed to have a public defender made available, but asked, "Do you have a lawyer?"

Rios just shook his head, but did not deny his participation in the prostitution ring. "But," he said, "I didn't kill those two girls."

"Then who did kill them?" Colby asked.

"Santos," Rios replied.

"Was he your partner?" Colby pushed, "Better tell us more about Mr. Santos; what is his first name? What you say better be the truth, it is in your own interest," Jim Colby strongly asserted.

Rios was almost choking, spoke in a half whisper. "It's Hugo Santos; we did everything together, whatever Mr. J. wanted. Santos never liked his name, always went by just Santos."

Colby interrupted Rios; "Is Mr. J. the lawyer, Jake Jacoby?"

"Yes sir, he was our boss, paid us well, in cash."

"I doubt if you will think that it was well enough by the time you spend a few years in prison," Colby jibbed; the Lieutenant nodded in agreement.

"Anyway," Rios continued, "I never carried a gun, just a knife. Santos did, and a knife. When we found out that those two girls had Herpes and Aids, we didn't know what to do with them. Mr. J. said that we couldn't peddle them and we couldn't just let them go. If they told anyone, he said, even the Mexicans, they would lead the police right back to us. He said to get rid of them; Santos volunteered; he really liked to shoot that gun. He said that it was registered, but I doubt it."

"What about the gun; does Santos have it?" Colby asked.

"Maybe, but he told Jacoby that he had dumped it in the middle of Lake Odell, and that because of the mud bottom it would never be found. Knowing Santos though, I can't see him throwing away anything worth several hundred dollars. My guess is that he still has it."

"Did you, Santos, and Jacoby all have lunch at the Lone Pine Restaurant prior to the murders?" Colby asked.

"Yea, we did," Rios said, "that was when we scouted the forest area after meeting in that Pinewood cabin. We told a few nosy people that we were just looking at lots to possibly build a cabin."

"Where is Santos?"

"Should be in California, the San Francisco area, at his sister's."

"Do you know the sister's name, address, or anything that would help us locate Santos in California?"

"No; I only heard Santos refer to her as his sister; never gave a name."

"Well Ziggy," Colby went on, "you have a problem. We have to find Santos, take him into custody, and then get evidence that he was the one who killed the girls. If we fail, then you're on the hook." Rios looked as though he was going to throw up; he went white and squirmed in his chair.

"Now what about Jacoby, where is he?" Colby asked.

"I don't know. He was supposed to be here today to post bail for me, if they let me out."

"Forget that, Rios. I think that your leader may already be in Mexico...or somewhere else. Better forget him; you'll see him soon, right here, I promise you."

CHAPTER THIRTY SIX

In the evidence room in Phoenix, the technicians were continuing to examine and re-examine the dead girls' clothes, which included the skimpy sandals that both of them had worn. One of the sandals had been better preserved than the others; it had been stuffed between the knees of one of the victims, or just thrown in at the last second of the burial. It had been put aside when the clothes were brought in and the concentration had been on the cloth materials. As the lab technician carefully brushed off the dried dirt from the one sandal, she uncovered a slim paper item. She removed it, cleaned it meticulously, and found that she was looking at a "Robert Burns" cigar band. She immediately put in a call for the initial detective team.

Orsen Carter took the fragile cigar band from the technician's hand and carefully held it closer to a nearby lamp, with partner Wes Mitzer looking over his shoulder, he turned and asked Wes, "Didn't Millie say that one of the men in the trio that lunched at the restaurant had an unlit cigar in his hand?"

"I forgot about that, but I think that it is in one of our notes. As I recall now, she said that the reason she remembered that incident was because she had to tell him that smoking was not allowed at inside tables."

"This could be the key that unlocks the door to convicting Jacoby, if we ever find him," Orsen optimistically stated. "Let's call Colby to get the okay to search Jacoby's residence and his office; we need some connection between the cigar band and Jacoby, more than Millie's statement. We'll probably have to get warrants for the searches, even if Jacoby has flown the coop. I'll call Jim right now."

Colby had the warrants ready when Carter and Mitzer came to pick them up. His spirits were riding high after Carter had told him about the cigar band over the phone. "Well I have some good news too," he said enthusiastically, "we have solved another piece of the puzzle. The Barstow squad finally found the license plate of the sedan at the scene of the accident. The number was traced to the owner of the car, a Ken Wade, whose car was stolen by his neighbor, Hugo Santos, the man Ziggy Rios said killed Frankie Salvo and the Mexican girls. He was incinerated in the accident and his entire ID was destroyed. However, there is no question that it was him, but forensics will still try for double confirmation through some of his teeth that were found and skull and other bone fragments. That should settle the Santos question. If we can locate his sister in California, as a matter of courtesy, we will have her notified of her brother's death. I'll leave that to the authorities there. Now we have to concentrate on Jacoby, so go do your searches."

The team decided to split up, to save time, and Carter chose to investigate the office, and Mitzer took the warrant for the residence, an apartment in west Chandler. The apartment had scant furniture; there was little clothing in the closets; the refrigerator held rancid milk, which Mitzer put down the kitchen drain; a pile of old mail was on the floor; in all it had the appearance of a poor bachelor's abode. The one bedroom was a mess; the bed was well over due for a change of linen. It didn't take Mitzer long to complete the search of the apartment for any material item that would assist the detectives in making a connection with the cigar band or anything else. He called Carter on his cell phone and was instructed to come to Jacoby's office.

Carter had a more pleasant experience at the office; it was fairly clean, although it too, was sparsely furnished. There was a wood desk of moderate size, two filing cabinets, a small computer that sat on a stand behind the desk, an "executive's" chair and two modest conference chairs. A combination work station and reception area fronted the small office, obviously used as a secretary's area, which also had little more than a small typing desk and chair. Carter checked out the filing cabinets first and found nothing of importance; then he started to examine the desk, starting with the top middle drawer and then worked down to the lower drawers. He was surprised to find so little paper work, knowing that most lawyers generate piles of paper. In the lower right-hand drawer he was more successful. As he greeted Mitzer at the office door, he said, "Guess what I found."

Mitzer looked at it and beamed, "I can't believe it, a box of "Robert Burns" cigars!"

CHAPTER THIRTY SEVEN

Lake Odell sits just behind the 12th green of the Pinewood Country Club golf course, but it is not part of the course. Upon viewing it for the first time one is apt to question the title of "Lake," because it is not of lake dimensions. In times of drought it often shrinks to a modest pond size, or less. It is saucer-like in shape, with the center being the deepest part, plunging to a mere six feet when full...which isn't very often.

True, the lake does have somewhat of a muddy bottom, but it still provides an ample variety of small fish for the anglers, most of whom are local boys who fish from the shore...when there is sufficient water to support fish.

A resident independent contractor, Carl Muntz, has been used from time to time to retrieve golf balls from the small ponds that are part of the country club's golf course. When the Phoenix police learned that the gun used to kill Frankie Salvo may have been disposed of in Lake Odell, Carl Muntz was hired to search the lake for the gun.

It was still quite cold for late March, and a full wet suit was required for Muntz to do the bottom search. The dragline he used first failed to pull anything in but cast-off items that some non-environmentally minded locals had tossed into the lake.

Although the temperature at 7000 feet was only in the high forties, the sun was shining brightly, providing good vision right down to the bottom of the lake. Carl also had the benefit of having been hired previously to search the lake; once when a Canadian woman visiting friends in Pinewood dropped a watch over the side of a canoe. It was a small lady's watch, but he found it. He was probably more familiar with the bottom of the lake than anyone else. He benefited his searches by trying to learn as much as possible about the circumstances leading up to the loss of an item in the lake, thus avoiding the waste of time and effort in conducting the search in unlikely areas.

When Muntz got the assignment and learned that the lost item was a gun, he knew immediately that it was probably thrown out from the shoreline beyond the knoll in back of the 12th green. There were no cabins or other structures in that area, thus fairly isolated from any casual observer. Any other area would not have provided any secrecy for someone disposing of anything in the lake. Those considerations permitted Muntz to concentrate on a triangular area of the lake leading out from the throwing point he had determined.

As he entered the cold water he recalled the information he had received, which included the words, "the gun may or may not be in the lake," not a happy thought. Only his pleasure of working under water urged him on...that and the bonus he was promised if he found the gun.

Muntz decided early that he would go out on a straight line from the speculated throwing point toward the center of the lake. There had been little activity in and around the lake since last fall, so the bottom had seen a minimum of disturbance. Muntz used a small handled garden rake and methodically made six slow sweeps on the floor of the lake, starting on his left side and moving to his right after each sweep, up to the where he thought might be about the middle of the lake.

He had found nothing but trash and was discouraged, knowing that he would have to go back to the shore and start a new work area, to the right or left of where he started his first search. As he drew his rake toward himself on the last sweep, he felt a scrape; he put his head right down to where the rake head had struck something. He brushed away a thin layer of mud that covered a metal object...a gun. He smiled broadly behind his face mask.

CHAPTER THIRTY EIGHT

At the DiBiasi cabin in Pinewood, Detective Neil Carpenter turned on every light in the house after tripping the circuit breaker. He had been given just one assignment: find an expended bullet or shell case. His instructions included a description, given over the phone by Jim Colby, of how he believed that the two girls had been shot.

"As I envision the scene," Jim had said, "the two girls were most likely tied to chairs before they were shot. That would give the killer, or killers, a straight shot at their hearts. Had they been standing, they would probably have turned away from the threat and would have been shot somewhere other than through their hearts." Colby had previously told Neil that the medical examiner had explained that the girls were so small and emaciated that the bullets had traveled right through their thin bodies. Colby had suggested that there might be marks or wear on chairs in the cabin that would indicate that someone had been restrained in those chairs. Beyond passing on those suggestions, he knew that Detective Carpenter had years of experience and would apply his own imagination as to where he might find evidence of the shootings.

After a slow walk through every room, including the upstairs bedrooms, Carpenter dismissed all of the four bedrooms as unlikely locations for the evil deed, the kitchen was also excluded. That left the great room, or family room, as the preferable location; there were two regular, straight-up chairs, a large closed sofa bed with two matching "soft" chairs, and a wood rocker. He eliminated all but the two straight-up chairs, which had vertical spokes that framed the backs. Examining the first chair, he saw a small chip in the side of one of the spokes that exposed the raw wood.

The detective observed that behind the two chairs, which were a fair distance out from the north wall, there was centered a stone fireplace topped by a thick mantle of dark wood. The Mantle was about two and a half inches thick and ran about four feet across. He checked out the second chair, but found it clear of any damage.

Returning to the first chair, he lined it up to the mantle, starting from the chipped back spoke, using a large metal measuring tape; there was no mark on the dark wood at that point. He took out his small strong pencil flashlight and combed the front area. Hidden in a knotty section, he noted the glint of metal; with a little pocketknife he dug out what he believed to be a 38 slug.

In minutes he was on his cell phone and talking to Jim Colby. "Hey boss," he greeted Colby, "I thought that you would like to know right away; I dug what looks like a 38 slug out of the wood mantle here at the DiBiasi cabin. It's beaten up pretty badly, but I think that the caliber could be determined. You were right on target with your suggestions."

"Okay, Neil, that's great. Bring it in right now. This case is getting to shape up. We were just delivered the gun that was thrown into Lake Odell, the one we believe was used in the killings; we're hoping to make a match with your slug."

Carpenter said, "I'm going to take another quick look around; might find the other bullet, then I'll head in after stopping at the

Lone Pine Restaurant for some hot coffee. It's still pretty cold up here, and this cabin has been like an ice box."

"That's fine, Neil; we'll look for you this afternoon," Colby agreed, and they hung up.

CHAPTER THIRTY NINE

The next morning, in Jim Colby's office, the prime detective team of Orsen Carter and Wes Mitzer sat and listened to the summary of the evidence in the case of against Jake Jacoby and Ziggy Rios. "You two and everyone in this case have done a great job," Colby said, "including those who were not paid to do so, such as our waitress gal, Millie, the body shop owner, Art Gibson, and others. The evidence group came through for us with the cigar band, and we got lucky with the gun and the bullet, which, incidentally, was matched just last night. I think that we are in great shape to move this case forward."

Detective Carter asked, "What about the defendants; how are they going to be named in the indictments, which I presume are in the works?"

"As you know," Colby replied, "Mr. Santos is dead, so we won't file anything on him, but he will still be mentioned in the indictments for his participation in the murder of the two girls, and he will be named as the guilty party in the death of Frank Salvo. We have established that the same gun was used in that crime by matching the bullet taken from Salvo's skull."

"Has Rios given us the whole story?" Mitzer inquired, "And is it credible?"

"I think we've got his story straight," Colby answered, "but even if he wavers, the testimony of Millie and Art Gibson, particularly about the pickup, should seal the case, even if he recants the confession he had made in hopes of some leniency."

"Guess that leaves us Jake Jacoby to worry about," Carter stated. "So far the APB hasn't generated anything, unless we haven't been told."

"No, we just haven't had a word, Orsen. I know, and I'm concerned about that, but it hasn't been out very long. I've reviewed the whole case with Mr. and Mrs. DiBiasi and they finally came around to understand that he is a criminal. They said that he had mentioned Mexico in the past and they knew that he had vacationed there, but I have discounted that destination for him; it's too predictable." Colby looked at his team; "Any ideas?"

"I know it is pretty close," Carter ventured, "but he probably has contacts in New Mexico that might help him blend into that society."

"There, and also California, Colby responded, but I have a hunch that he would want to get further away, maybe even to Canada. The border people up there should have been alerted by the APB, but I'm going to send photos of Jacoby with a special alert notice to Vancouver and Calgary, and also to some of the major stops stateside between here and the border. The APB reported his car, if he is still driving it, as a 2006 Lincoln Continental; should be easy to spot; and of course they have the license numbers. We have to think that he may have sold or ditched the car, and could be relying on bus or train transportation. I doubt if he would gamble flying; too much ID. I'd like you both to contact the appropriate parties at the bus companies and the railroads. We can't let this bastard get away. I'll let you know if the APB brings a response. Marsha will buzz you on your cell phone." He nodded to the team as they left.

CHAPTER FORTY

Jake Jacoby had settled his plumpish five-eight body into his Lincoln Continental with an almost eager anticipation of stopping off in Las Vegas. He had been there, several times, but was not a heavy gambler, a far cry from being a high roller. He liked the slots and pretty much stuck to the quarter machines, occasionally getting adventuresome and moving over to the dollar area. He had never lost much, but did have a good hit a few years back, for $5,000.

As he drove northwest on highway 93 toward Wickenburg he cracked his side window just a bit, unwrapped a Robert Burns cigar and lit it with the car's lighter. He actually felt a little smug and again envisioned the possibility of arranging something for some sexual pleasure in Las Vegas. "Unless I need gas," he thought, "I won't stop in Kingman. I'll have a cheapie dinner when I get to Vegas, and then enjoy the evening. Maybe spend two nights there, then get going on I-15 to Salt Lake City for one night; maybe hit Yellowstone before trying for the border." He knew that he could stay on I-15 all the way from Las Vegas.

He mulled over his past life while puffing away on his cigar: the unsavory characters he had worked for after passing the Arizona Bar exam, all because of an introduction by a former classmate at ASU. The money had been good then, tainted, but good. It stopped when some of his clients wound up in prison. Then there was his failed marriage; his fault. He reflected back to those early days when he never saw a skirt that didn't entice him to follow it. "Good thing we never had any kids," he mused as he moved along the highway. Traffic was light for a Tuesday early afternoon.

Jacoby was calm, turned on some country music on the car radio and continued the mental re-hash of his fifty-four years of life. "Frankie Salvo was a problem," he admitted, "I just didn't see it soon enough. I should have known better than to team up with a drinker/gambler, especially after having those early clients that almost got me disbarred," he reflected. "Ziggy and Santos were okay," he continued, "it was really Gonzales and Garcia that screwed us up."

The drive to Las Vegas went quickly and smoothly, with Jacoby suddenly realizing that he was driving down the strip, ogling the short-skirted pedestrians while trying to decide what motel or casino he should check into. It didn't take him long to apply some common sense into his selection; he was a legal aberration, but he did have above average intelligence; he eliminated the high profile casinos and chose a motel at the cheap end of the strip, the Lucky Winner.

Hunger grabbed his first attention after parking his car and checking in, so he settled for a light meal at the motel snack bar; they had no restaurant. Then he looked for some pleasure; took a cab for a short ride to the nearest casino, not one that was name-famous. He went straight to the dollar slots, ordered a vodka-tonic from the drink girl who hit on him as soon as he sat down and started the wheel turning. When the girl returned with his drink he tipped her a dollar; holding unto her hand for a second as he gave her the money, he said with a lecherous grin, "I just got into town; do you know where I might get lucky tonight?" She knew what he meant, and hesitated, not wishing to be rude to this portly, thin-haired, middle-aged customer.

She gave him a be-nice-to-the customers' smile, and answered, slowly withdrawing her hand from his: "Well I'm new here," she lied, "but I'll see what I can do, will check back with you a little later." That seemed to satisfy him.

"Fine," Jacoby replied, returning to his machine. He took a long slug of his drink, and then said to no one, "Okay, now let's see what we can do here." He had selected a dollar progressive machine, one which continued to increase the total big jackpot pay out with successive amounts wagered. The wheel turned over and over with Jacoby clenching his fists as time after time his combinations just missed a pay back. He was getting unhappy, the drink girl hadn't returned, with or without another vodka-tonic or news about companionship for the evening.

Luck did come to him just about the time he was ready to quit the machine; he didn't get the big one, but he won what some casino customers call a "teaser" jackpot, $10,000, which brought out all the bells and whistles, and a two person staff committee that ushered him to the Cashier. After all of the details were confirmed, Jacoby asked for $3,000 in cash and the balance, after the IRS take, to be in a check. The cashier dispensing the money questioned Jacoby about whether he was sure about taking the $3,000 in cash. He assured her that that was what he wanted, so she complied.

With at least a partially successful first outing, Jacoby cheerfully left the casino and began a quest for a Chinese restaurant; it wasn't the best for his body because he always ate too much, but he loved the egg rolls. He hailed a cab and solicited a recommendation from the driver, who said that he also loved Chinese food. "Enjoy your dinner," the cabby said as he dropped Jacoby off at the China Gate Restaurant.

Jacoby started with a glass of Merlot, and then indulged in the egg roll and combination plate he had ordered, until he could eat no more. He finished with another glass of wine, which then had him drift into a melancholy state. His brain became crowded with regrets…with what might have been. He roused himself sufficiently enough to pay his bill, leaving a generous tip, in cash.

As Jacoby left the restaurant, he was pleased to see a cab at the curb almost in front of the restaurant's front door. Without looking inside, he opened the back door; before he was halfway into the cab he was grabbed by his shirt and hauled bodily into the car. He was frightened and could only muster a weak "What the hell!" After which he knew nothing; he had been knocked unconscious.

When he came to, he was alone in the taxi, which had parked in front of the Treasure Island casino, and as usual, there were crowds of people waiting for the next sinking of the pirate ship. Some of the spectators had gathered around the taxi, looking at him through the windows and asking, "Are you okay mister?" Or, "Do you need help?"

As Jacoby shook off the fog in his brain he reached a hand up to the back of his head and felt a wet spot that covered a knob the size of small egg. The blood was nearly dry. At the same time he realized that he had been set up by the cabbie that took him to the restaurant. He roused himself enough to be able to open the car door, and exited half stumbling into the arms of a male spectator. "Sorry," he said as he tried to extricate himself from the stranger's arms, "I've been robbed. My wallets gone, my money's gone." The men and women nearby heard that and voiced their alarm. One quickly dialed 911, while others asked if he needed a doctor, or if they could help him.

He quieted himself and answered, "No, I'm fine," and began to walk unsteadily away from the area. The spectators returned their attention to the action on the pirate ship.

A block away, Jacoby continued to walk, unaware of where he was or where he was going. A police car, in response to the 911 call, came toward him, passed him half a block, and then returned, pulling up to the curb just in front of his path.

Officer Randy Berko stepped out of the passenger's side of the vehicle and put his hand on Jacoby's chest, helping to steady the wobbly man; "Sir, did you just leave a cab in front of the Treasure Island Casino?"

Jacoby looked blank, his head throbbing. "I was robbed," he blubbered, "back there somewhere," he pointed roughly behind him. "Got my wallet, my cash, everything. It was the cabbie; he knocked me out."

The officer said, rather without any emotion, "I'm sorry. We'll get the details of that from you in a minute, but first, are you okay? Do you need a doctor?"

"No, no, I hurt, but I'm okay," Jacoby answered, "But what about my money?"

Officer Berko looked questioningly at Jacoby, "Are you local, or are you visiting tourist?"

"Just visiting; I'm on my way to Salt Lake City to visit friends," Jake replied, his head starting to clear a bit.

The officer asked, "How did you get here? Did you fly, or did you drive up here? If you drove, did you come up from Phoenix? If you did drive, what kind of vehicle were you driving and where is it?"

Jacoby began to perspire; he started to feel that the officer was pushing him for answers to too many questions, causing him to become apprehensive. In spite of his slightly inebriated condition he tried to remain calm as he replied to the questions. "It's just an old Lincoln Continental, parked by my motel."

Berko's partner came up to him at that point, "Just got this off the screen," he said. "Randy, look at this APB picture, then look at your man there."

Officer Randy Berko looked at the picture and at the accompanied data relative to the Lincoln Continental, and then turned to the pudgy, sweating, nervous man in front of him, and asked: "Are you Jake Jacoby?"

Jacoby was white as a snowdrift, his head hurt, his head was lowered, and in a quivering whisper, he answered.

"Yes."

CHAPTER FORTY ONE

The convictions went smoothly; the public defenders could offer no creditable evidence to substantiate the innocent pleas that Jacoby and Rios had entered. There were no friends or family members of either defendant present to make a plea for leniency. They were, then, given the maximum sentences: life imprisonment with no opportunity for parole. Everyone involved in the three cases believed that the sentences were fair for Frankie Salvo's murder (Rios had been named as an accessory to the crime), the trafficking of women for the purpose of prostitution, and the murder of the two Mexican girls. The Mexican authorities were pleased with the outcome of the prostitution case and the resulting improved relationship with Arizona that pointed toward a lessening of young girls involved in prostitution on both sides of the border.

In the home of Emil and Rosemary DiBiasi almost the entire family gathered together in the family room. Mama and Papa sat upright in their respective recliners; Gus (minus his tic) and Elaine sat in simple straight chairs on each end of the long sofa; Lucy held baby Frankie on the sofa, where she patted him gently while he slept; Jean and Connie were on either side of Lucy and the baby; Al and Jerry occupied themselves with the delivering a glass of red wine to each of them…Al pouring and Jerry making the deliveries. Connie's husband, Dick, was tied up at the laundromat and none of the three grandchildren were able to be present.

When everyone had received a glass of wine they held unto it until the patriarch Emil, in his customary manner at family gatherings, would propose a toast, of sorts. Although basically a religious man, he saved his prayers for Sundays at church; he liked to have happy faces and joyous laughter, which he believed was brought forth by good red wine.

"We have been through some difficult times," Emil started as he raised his glass, "but this is to the future and better times." Everyone nodded and tasted of their wine. Emil continued, "We thought that we only had a problem about our cabin, but it turned out to be much more, sadly. Mama and I have been talking about the cabin since those terrible crimes were solved. We believe that the cabin is no longer the happy place that we knew for so many years. The crimes that were committed there have cast a shadow on it; we don't believe that we, or any of you, could enjoy the cabin in the future because of what happened there." Emil paused and took another sip of his wine.

"What are you trying to tell us, Papa?" Jerry interjected. "Are you saying that you have decided to sell the cabin?"

Emil breathed deeply for a second, wishing that he did not have to respond with the answer that he and Rosemary had already agreed upon. "Exactly," he finally blurted out.

"But what about the taxes that will have to be paid?" Jerry questioned.

"I know, they will be pretty hefty, but Mama and I think that it is the thing to do,"

Emil answered; "It solves the problem ahead of time, for all of you, and we can afford the taxes, thanks to some extent to Al's guiding our investments over the years. So as soon as the cabin is sold, and until the net monies received from the sale are exhausted, we can give all of you some substantial cash, at a time of your lives when you can use it the most. The day after the sale

I will be writing a check for $10,000 to each of you, to start with. Now, does anyone have an objection to that?"

"Not me," someone said; "I'm happy," another chimed in; "That solves a lot of problems," a third voiced his feelings... followed by nods and murmurs of consent.

"Well then," Papa Emil happily proposed, raising his glass again, "Here is to our new grandson, Frankie, Jr., to our darling daughter Lucy, and to all of you who make up the DiBiasi family."

They all tilted up their glassed and drained them dry. Papa then said, "Okay Al and Jerry, do your duty again. "Let's celebrate the sale of Gus's pharmacy business and his new job with the Westwind Hospital, then let's discuss who is going to win the Suns game Saturday night."